A FACE IN THE MIRROR

K. L. Keeley

'If history were taught in the form of stories, it would never be forgotten'

– Rudyard Kipling

CHAPTER ONE

The hustle and bustle of everyday life in London was daunting for the two young boys, as they sat on the steps of their new large Victorian-style home. Even in their street; Cornwall Gardens which was situated in a quieter part of the city near the Natural History Museum, it was still loud and busy and as far from their lovely little cottage in Ludwig as you could get. The boys missed the taste of salt in the air and the ice wind that slapped your face, as you ran along the beach of the Jurassic coast looking for fossils. The closest they could get to fossils now was peering at them through a glass cabinet at the museum that their mother and father had promised to take them to once they had unpacked.

'Do you think we will ever get used to it?' Sighed Alfie, as a car beeped loudly as it zoomed past. Even though their street was two miles away from the main road, it sounded like the cars where right outside their gate.

'I don't want to get used to it' replied Jack angrily 'I want to go home!'

Alfie rolled his eyes, he understood his younger brother's frustration, but he also knew that there was not much point complaining about it. The boy's father was a politician and had been asked by the new Prime Minister; Jerome Calvin, to be his home secretary. It was an amazing opportunity for their father and Alfie had known instantly that it would have meant a move to London, as soon as his mother and father had sat him and Jack down and excitedly told them the good news. Alfie didn't want to be the one to destroy his father's dreams and so had smiled and kept his mouth shut as he packed away his room, and waved goodbye to the cottage and the sea that he loved. His brother, on the other hand, had moaned and cried from the second he had been informed, making the three-hour car journey even more unbearable.

'At least we are close to the museum; I didn't expect the house to be this close' smiled Alfie, as he leaned out of the way of one of the men dad had hired to help them move in. The man carried a large box up the steps to the house, a small vein popping out of the side of his neck as he struggled under the weight.

'Please, please be careful!' A small, frantic woman shouted as she ran through the hall, passing the struggling man. 'My late grandmother's antique china is in that box and she will turn in her grave if it is chipped'.

The two boys giggled. Their poor mother had not taken the move very well either, she was incredibly stressed and kept glaring at the removal men with a look of disdain every time they lingered in the back of the van for too long and emerged sometime later covered in biscuit crumbs. 'Lazy sods' she kept mumbling under her breath.

'Yeah I am glad about that' said Jack turning back to Alfie 'I'm really excited to see the dinosaurs; they are supposed to have an amazing collection of fossils. Plus, the Victoria and Albert museum is right next door'.

The two boys smiled; they had always been fond of history an interest they had inherited from their mother and her mother before her, who had both been high school history teachers.

'Have you picked your rooms?' Their father asked as his smiling face popped out from around the corner of the door. Jack was the first to jump up, although he was not enthusiastic about the idea of having a new room; he was far too competitive to allow his brother to beat him up the staircase.

Red-faced and gasping Alfie arrived at the top of the stairs to find Jack sat smirking at him from a chair randomly placed in the middle of the large landing. The Victorian house was very grand with 3 double bedrooms and a smaller single room that was to be used as dad's office. There were six doors on the landing 3 belonged to the bedrooms, one was for the office and the other a spacious bathroom with a claw foot bath that sat in the tiled room's centre. The two boys stood outside the sixth door looking a mixture of excited and apprehensive; they had no idea what lay behind it.

'Open it' whispered Jack, his untidy brown hair slightly damp with sweat from the run-up the staircase.

'If it's a fourth bedroom and it's bigger than the others, whoever opens it automatically claims it' laughed Alfie as Jack jumped to grab the handle before he had even finished the sentence.

The old heavy door creaked open and revealed a dusty, wooden staircase. The two brothers stepped forward; a cloud of dust escaping from under their trainers as they stood on the faded red carpet that lay on the stairs. It smelt old and musty and the dust made the boys cough as they inhaled it into the back of their throats.

'This must be the attic mum was telling me about' said Alfie 'she said it's huge, big enough for a game room' excitement filled their chests as they continued up the steps.

Halfway up there was a light switch on the wall. Alfie flicked it and a light at the top of the stairs came on and revealed another heavy wooden door, a replica of the one below. Alfie reached out and turned the porcelain handle, he pushed his shoulder against the door and the door burst open with a jolt. The room that lay before them was huge; it covered the whole size of the second floor of the house. There were dusty cardboard boxes dotted about; some had moth-eaten clothes and other fabrics in. One box was filled with picture frames; the black and white faces that looked back at Jack as he held the antique frames in his hand scared him.

'Do you think any of these people died in this house?' He whispered to his brother, his voice cracking as he tried to sound braver than he felt.

'Probably' shrugged Alfie as he continued to root through boxes and old suitcases. 'Wow look at these Halloween decorations' he shouted excitedly as he pulled out a large skeleton that was hanging from a dark brown cord rope, and an emerald green velvet witches hat that had a thick black belt around the rim, and a large shiny black buckle in the centre. Jack paid no attention he had just spotted what could only be described as a pirate's treasure chest, sat at the back of the attic, hidden in a dark corner. His heart pounded as images of gold coins and jewels filled his head. He crawled over to the chest and blew away the dust that blanketed the large metal square on the front of it. A small keyhole appeared and Jack crossed his fingers as he placed his hands on the lid and prayed it was not locked. He pushed up and with a loud squeak of its joints, the chest lid opened. Alfie's head rose as he heard the noise and he looked across the room towards his brother.

'Cool that looks like a pirate's chest' he said as he stood and walked across the attic to where Jack and the chest sat. Jack peered into the chest and his face dropped. There was no treasure just some old records from the 60s, a few pictures of a man and woman from different stages of their life; their wedding, a holiday to the beach with their young baby and the same couple but old and smiling into the camera from behind glasses that framed their wrinkled faces. There was a set of silver candlesticks and a wooden box. Alfie reached into the chest and picked up the box, he removed the lid and inside was a silk scarf; it was a beautiful shade of sky blue with a golden pattern embroidered into it. Alfie stroked the silk it was soft and smelt like spring flowers. He attempted to pull the scarf out of the box and then he realised it was wrapped around something hard and heavy. Carefully he unwrapped the scarf from the object and held out a stunning gold hand mirror. The mirror was oval-shaped with jewels embedded all around it; the handle had hieroglyphics carved into it and every gem and precious jewel that you could think of. The emeralds, rubies, diamonds and jade twinkled in the light from the window above.

'That has to be fake' laughed Jack as he looked at his brother's shocked face 'there is no way the jewels are real; they are probably just costume jewellery'.

'How dare you' shouted a woman's voice.

The two boys froze with fear. Where had that voice came from, it didn't sound like their mothers and there wasn't anybody else in the attic with them. Baffled they turned to each other, but before either of them could ask if the other had also heard the voice, it spoke again.

'Costume jewellery, well I have never….in all my years…. the cheek of it!'

Alfie dropped the mirror in fright, he was sure this time the voice had come from it, he had wondered at first maybe it was a trick his ears had played, but now he was sure of it….the mirror could talk!

'Ouch. Oh, dear boy please do be more careful I am incredibly old and fragile you cannot just throw me about like that' the mirror gasped.

Jack unfroze and made a bolt for the door.

'Wait' shouted his brother 'Jack wait. This is mental! It can't be true mirrors don't talk. Please don't go it's probably a trick of some sort. Come and sit down with me it will be ok let's just try and figure out what's going on.' Jack stopped and turned to his brother, but he was too scared to move any closer. Alfie picked up the mirror once more and looked at his own reflection.

'Sorry Mrs Mirror' he replied. He had tried to make his voice sound like a laugh, but the fear had crept through, so it was more of a croak. Suddenly his reflection changed; his eyes which were normally round with thick black eyelashes and as green as grass were now almond-shaped with thick black eyeliner that made them appear almost cat-like and as brown as oak, his small button nose was much more elegant and feminine, his chubby childlike cheeks were now sculptured and he had high sharp cheekbones. On his head sat a beautiful diadem encrusted in diamonds and entwining out and up from the centre were two silver cobras with small Jade stones for eyes. His normally blonde hair was jet black and thick; it fell to his shoulders and he had a thick black fringe that covered his whole forehead. His ears and neck were coated in jewels. It took only a second for him to realise he was no longer looking at himself, but a beautiful Egyptian woman.

'My name is Meritamen, not Mrs Mirror' the Egyptian woman snapped. She stared at Alfie as if trying to figure him out, she looked at his haircut and his clothes then she looked around the little of the room that she could see before turning back to him and asking 'what is the year my child?'

Alfie did not reply; he was petrified, his mind went blank; he did not know what to think or say or do.

This whole time Jack had been stood in the background watching from afar, he had gasped when he seen Meritamen's face appear, he had thought about running and it had taken him a few seconds to gather his thoughts, but he had quickly decided that it was not a trick, it was magic and that had intrigued him enough to help him shake his fear and step forward. He sat next to his brother and looked into the beautiful eyes of the Egyptian lady trapped in the mirror. She was very attractive; he could not find the words to describe how attractive and before he could stop himself, he had gasped 'you're so beautiful' before looking away blushing. His brother looked at him and laughed and like that all the tension had melted away and the situation, although completely bizarre somehow felt more relaxed.

'It is two thousand and seventeen' Alfie said, turning back to Meritamen.

'Ahh' she sighed.

'Why are you sad?' asked Jack shocking himself with the sympathy he felt for this strange lady that had just appeared in the mirror.

'Well my child, I have been in this box hidden away for over fifty years. I have been very lonely, and I fear now, that my last owner may no longer be of this earth. I shall miss her greatly; she was a very elegant lady with a kind heart.'

Alfie reached into the box and picked up one of the frames with the picture of the elderly couple inside.

'Was this your owner?' he asked, showing Meritamen the photograph.

A gentle smile appeared on her face.

'Yes child, that is my Annie. Thank you. Such a lovely lady. Not as fair of face as I, of course, but still, exceptionally beautiful in her own way'.

Alfie blinked in shock, but it was Jack that laughed and said.

'Bloody hell you're not modest are you'.

Meritamen smiled.

'Well young sir I have been raised in the light of the Goddess Hathor, those who are worthy to worship in her light need not be modest. I know I am beautiful because beauty is the gift, I received at birth from the Goddess herself. There are few that have ever compared to my beauty, but in my many years I have discovered that being fair in face is not everything. I have been owned by many inspiring, amazing women. Each has taught me something new, each has given me a different piece of wisdom, a different story to tell, so I have learnt that being a beautiful person does not mean having a beautiful face; it is to have a beautiful soul. Annie had a beautiful soul. I have been blessed to have been owned by many women who possessed this trait.'

The two boys stood and pulled a small table from the corner of the attic over to where the chest sat, they found some books in a dusty box and placed them on the table before balancing the mirror against them and sitting back onto the floor where they could sit comfortably and continue their chat.

'Is that better is it? Was your hand becoming sore? Am I really that heavy?' Meritamen laughed.

'It's all your jewels' laughed Alfie 'they weigh a tonne after a bit'.

Jack shuffled uncomfortably on the spot he peered up at the mirror, threw his thick eyelashes.

'If you don't mind me asking Meritamen, how did you end up in a hand mirror?'

Meritamen smiled kindly and gave a small cough for effect.

'Well my dear' she said, 'if I am to tell you my story, I feel it best to start from the beginning.'

CHAPTER TWO

'I was born in twelve hundred BC in Egypt, in the 19th Dynasty. My father was Ramesses ii, my mother Nefertari. They were both great leaders my father is known as Ramesses the great and my mother his great royal wife. I was raised in Abu Simbel, along with my brothers and sisters. We were wealthy and happy. My father was a prolific builder he built many great building and temples like the Ramesseum in Thebes and the massive rock temple in Abu Simbel. He was a great military warrior and we had many enemies like the Hittites, Nubians and Libyans. They tried to defeat my father and his army so they could take control of our lucrative trade routes along the Nile River. There was a great battle; the battle of Kadesh. My mother, sisters and I were so worried as my father went to battle along with my brother Prince Prehirwenemef. We thanked the Gods when they safely returned after securing our borders and suppressing the threat of our enemies. My mother died in twelve fifty-five BC and I became Great Royal Wife to my father.'

'WHAT!' blurted Jack. 'You married your dad! That's gross'

Meritamen gave a sigh.

'Please child, times where different then. We married within our families to keep our bloodline pure we had many enemies who wanted our throne; we did not trust others outside our family. So, by marrying within it, we secured our rights to the throne'.

Alfie stared at Jack with a look that said SHUTUP!!

'Make sense.' He said, turning to Meritamen with a tone of apology in his voice 'please carry on'.

Meritamen smiled, she knew that reaction was coming; she had told her story many times before and the reaction was always the same. Although she noted as the years had passed the reaction had become more dramatic, as people were becoming less and less accustomed to the way marriages use to be.

'Now where was I up to' she said with a smile. 'Ah yes. I became Great Royal Wife' she noticed Jack shudder, but she chose to ignore it. 'My half-sister Bintanath became Great Royal Wife along with me and we became very close after that even more so than before. I was my father's favourite; he had many statues created of me and placed them all over Egypt. He would use only the finest of Limestone and so I was known as "The White Queen". He would hold parties and gatherings in my honour so I could dance and sing for our guests. I played the Sistrum of Mut and the Menat necklace of Hathor and I would dance to worship her. My people loved me they would say I was fair of face and very well-spoken and that these traits were gifts off Hathor herself, because I pleased her so with my music and dancing. I was named a dancer of Hathor and became her priestess; my people would come to me to worship her and I would dance with them so that my Goddess would listen to their prayers and bless them. My father died in twelve thirteen BC and as I was his favourite Royal wife, I was to die with him. I was given a poison to drink after my father's death so that we could be reunited in the afterlife' Meritamen held back a sob.

'It's ok' whispered Alfie gently 'you don't have to carry on. That must have been terrible for you and I wouldn't want you to retell your horror. Let's talk about something else.'

'I can't believe they had to kill you just because your dad died, that's so mean. I would have come back to haunt them all if that was me!' shouted Jack angrily, he felt sorry for his new friend and the torture she must have gone through and was glad he did not live in a time where people were treated like objects.

Meritamen gave a slight smile.

'No children, I am not sad about my death you misunderstand. I knew my role; I do not fear death not even now. I am sad about my afterlife. I did not meet my father in the Promised Land; I did not go on to greater things and join the Gods like all the kings and queens before me. I was trapped inside this mirror for eternity where I have been tormented by life and where at times I have begged and pleaded for the God Anubis to take me. I have a lonely existence I am not alive, yet my soul is trapped in this object as it has been since twelve thirteen BC'.

The two boys sat awestruck the weight of their pity heavy in their hearts.

'That's an awfully long time' whispered Jack sadly. 'Is there any way we can help you, to free your soul?'

The door at the bottom of the attic stairs creaked open and their father's voice trailed up towards them.

'Boys are you up there?' He shouted.

'Yes, dad we're here' the two boys replied together.

'Ok, well mum is making tea now and you need to show me who's having what room so I can bring your boxes up' dad continued.

'Ok, we will be down now' shouted Alfie, he then turned to the mirror and smiled at Meritamen. He was not sure why, but in this short time he had become very fond of her. 'Listen we have to go now, but I won't put you back in the box; you can stay on the table and I'll move you over to by the window. Once our rooms are unpacked and there is less chance of mum and dad finding you or you getting broken, you can come down to our bedrooms. Is that ok?'

Meritamen beamed at the young fair-haired boy who stood before her. She had worried she would be going back into the box; after fifty years it had gotten rather claustrophobic.

'That sounds splendid, thank you' she replied.

Jack and Alfie moved the table over to a small circular window in the far end of the attic; which looked out onto the front garden below. The view this high up was spectacular, Meritamen could see right over the chimneys of the facing houses, and in the distance, the top of Big Ben and the millennium wheel could be seen. The boys made sure the mirror was stable against the books before saying their goodbyes, promising to come back the next day and heading down the stairs.

'I have just thought' said Jack

'Oh gosh that's worrying' laughed Alfie

'Shut up' giggled Jack. 'Seriously, do you want to share a room? Their big enough for our two beds and I was thinking when we do bring the mirror down, we would have to take turns who's room she was going to go in, so it just makes it easier doesn't it. We can pick the biggest room out of the three and both share it.' He added as he looked hopefully at his older brother. It had been a few years since the boys had shared a room; they use to argue terribly over the slightest little thing. In fact, it was only their mutual hatred towards the move to London that had united them the past few weeks and they had actually begun to get along.

'Mum and dad may faint when we tell them, but yes I think it makes sense' smiled Alfie as he put his arm around his little brother's shoulders 'come on roomy let's go pick out our room'.

CHAPTER THREE

The next morning the warm June sun beamed through the large bedroom window. The room was full of cardboard boxes not yet unpacked; half of the boxes had "Alfie's room" scribbled along their sides in permanent black marker, the others read "Jacks room". Two boys lay sleeping in their single beds placed against either wall of the room, the large window in-between them which looked out onto a spacious rear garden. The warmth from the sun shone onto the forehead of the sleeping fare haired boy, he moaned gently in his sleep and rolled onto his back; the sunlight now covering his whole face. He moaned again slightly louder and covered his face with his arm before sitting up dazed and looking around the room. Rubbing the sleep from his eyes, Alfie yawned loudly and looked over to his brother who lay, still snoring lightly in the bed next to his. What an odd first night in the new house they had had. The two boys had mentioned over dinner to their parents that they wanted to share a bedroom; the look their mother and father had given each other was a mixture of surprise, apprehension and happiness. Only time would tell if the choice was a good one, but the first night had gone well. They had helped dad carry their boxes and dismantled beds upstairs and chose the most spacious of the three rooms to have as theirs. Once their beds had been re-assembled the two brothers had been too tired to do any unpacking, so once they had dug out their bedding from the pile of boxes and bin bags that resembled a small mountain in the far corner, they had both jumped into bed and discussed the night's adventure in the attic before drifting off to sleep. Alfie's stomach lurched as he remembered what they had discovered in the attic the previous night. He leapt out of bed and darting across the room to wake his brother.

'Jack, Jack wake up!' he shook his brother vigorously.

Jack bolted upright a look of alarm etched across his face.

'WHAT! What's going on' he shouted in surprise. He looked up at his brother who lay over him still shaking his shoulders; a massive grin etched across his face.

'Alfie what do you want…..what time is it?' he added groggily.

'I'm not sure, but we need to get up Meritamen is waiting for us in the attic.'

Jacks heart began to race as he also remembered the previous night's adventure. He jumped up and started rooting through the many boxes for some clothes to put on, his brother next to him doing the same. Once dressed the two boys raced for the old wooden door that led to the attic stairs but just as Jack's hand reached for the large porcelain knob, their mother called up the stairs from the ground floor to announce that breakfast was ready. With a sigh, they turned disheartened and sloughed down the stairs to the kitchen. Their mother stood smiling at them when they walked into the kitchen/diner. The smell of scotch pancakes and maple syrup filled the air.

'How was your first night then guys?' she asked kindly as she lay a large overflowing plate of warm homemade pancakes down in the centre of the kitchen table. The boy's stomachs growled when the smell filled their nostrils; they hadn't realised how hungry they were. They both sat down and began to eat.

'It was good' mumbled Alfie through a mouthful of fluffy pancakes 'slept really well'. Their mother smiled and turned back to the sink to continue washing. She was a small, slim woman with long brown hair that she wore scraped back into a sleek ponytail. She had piercing blue eyes and long thick eyelashes that Jack had inherited. She sighed happily as she reached for a dishcloth to dry the dishes. She had worried so much about the move and how it would affect her sons. Henry had told her 'Rose don't worry once we are in and settled they will be fine', but she hadn't wanted to build her hopes up, and then the first night they had asked if they could share a room and all her tensions had lifted, perhaps this move would be good for them after all.

'Mum we're done, can we go and explore the house now?' asked jack.

'What already? That was quick, are you sure you're done?' Their mother asked suspiciously as she eyed the empty plates. 'Ok sure. Have fun.'

The two boys darted up the stairs and made a beeline for the attic door. The stairs creaked as they leapt up them and burst into the attic.

The mirror sat in the place where they had left it; propped up against some books on a small table in front of a circular-shaped window. Alfie reached out and picked the mirror up, turning it around slowly expecting to see the beautiful face of the ancient Egyptian lady trapped inside, but it was his own reflection that stared back at him.

'Well she's got to be in there somewhere' whispered Jack as he watched the look of disappointment spread across his brother's face.

'Meritamen?' whispered Alfie. Suddenly a beautiful face appeared in the mirror. Meritamen smiled at the two young boys looking eagerly back at her.

'How was your slumber?' she asked kindly.

'She means sleep' whispered Alfie to his younger brother as a look of confusion crossed his face.

'We slept really well thanks. How was your night? Did you enjoy having a view to look at last night?'

'Oh yes' beamed the Egyptian Queen 'I do appreciate what you did young man.'

'Can we hear the rest of the story, please?' asked Jack. He could not wait any longer he was so excited to find out how his new friend had become trapped in this handheld mirror all them years ago.

'I thought you would never ask' smiled Meritamen. 'Now, where was I? Ah yes, the poison. I should, however, mention that as members of the royal family, we had many slaves. The Ancient Egyptian's imprisoned Jews whom we kept as slaves, they built our buildings and tombs such as the Pyramids and our great temples. It was a terrible existence. They were worked to exhaustion and many Jews died during these times. Many years before I was born, my father had owned a young man and women. The man was a good strong worker. He had helped my father build many of his temples. Unbeknown to my father, this young man had taken another of my father's slaves; a young woman, as his wife. The young woman became pregnant and sadly died in childbirth. The child was raised by his father as best he could, but the young man was worked to exhaustion and sadly he also died, leaving his young son orphaned. A wealthy woman who secretly provided food to the slaves found the orphaned babe and took him home. She raised him as her own, giving him nice clothes and a good education. When he reached the age of manhood, his new mother told him of his troublesome start to life and the boy began to mourn the parents he had never known. Hatred consumed the young man and he hatched out a plan. He began to train with priests of Arum, he was a bright man and he learnt quickly. Soon he had risen to a powerful position within the church and before long he was requested upon by the Royal Family to bless their remains and give them safe passage to the afterlife. However, the priest did not fulfil their wishes; instead, he used black magic to entrap their soles into their most beloved items and imprisoned them into an existence of limbo. The worst punishment known to man and the most loneliness of existences, forever trapped inside our tombs in darkness and alone dreaming of the afterlife we so longed for.'

'Wait. So, you're telling me that dotted around the world there is talking mirrors like you with your family members trapped inside?' gasped Jack.

'I am telling you that yes, there are members of my family whose souls are imprisoned within artefacts they once treasured, much like me and my hand mirror. Whether they are dotted about the world is another matter. You see it was the Priests plan that I would be trapped in my tomb within the Valley of the Queens for all of time. But do you remember me telling you of my sister Bintanath? She was my best friend and my death brought her much sorrow. She came to my tomb before it was sealed to cry at my sarcophagus and say her final goodbyes. She seen my mirror placed on a table in the corner of my tomb and she remembered how I had often sat for hours looking at my reflection and brushing my hair. She became consumed within her grief and in a moment of madness, she took the mirror and fled. Bintanath could not cope with the guilt she felt for stealing my most favoured possession, how sad I would be, she thought, once I entered the afterlife and realised it was missing. She could not bring herself to look at the mirror and so she locked it in a drawer in her chambers. My sister had saved me, but alas she would never know, and her guilt consumed her life, she died young and depressed. Once she died, I was passed to our youngest of siblings Twosret and I soon learnt that I could appear in the mirror and talk to my owners. For this reason, I have been passed from person to person always looked after with the greatest of care, and although my heart is still heavy my existence is no longer dark, empty and lonely and for that, I am eternally grateful.'

'Wow' whispered Alfie 'that is crazy. So the priest used his black magic as a form of revenge. That is some hard-core passive-aggressiveness'.

'Wait! I have just had the craziest thought. Most of the tombs in the Valley of the Kings and queens have been excavated now and throughout history, there have been loads of cursed, magical or haunted items that have been recorded, well what if they're your family members trapped in their artefacts' gasped Jack.

'It is more than likely. You see my poor relatives would have been imprisoned inside their tombs for many hundreds of years before they were excavated and then probably passed around from scientists to archaeologists, before being locked away inside a museum somewhere. I would not be the slightest bit surprised if they were angry and beckoned on the Gods to curse those who handled them. I however, have lived a life; I have been cared for and loved, even worshipped. I have been asked for advice and in some ways, I have helped shape history. I have no reason to hold resentment to the people who have handled me as they have shown me great kindness.'

'So who has owned you?' asked Alfie intrigued.

'Oh many wonderful women, I have told you of my sisters Bintanath and Twosret. Once Twosret died I was owned by Claudia Procula who was the wife of an incredibly famous man named Pontius Pilot. I was then passed to her relative Pomponia Graecina; her husband was the Roman commander who led the invasion of Britain. After Pomponia, I was passed down from generation to generation. I showed myself to some and kept myself hidden from others. I then found a friend in the form of Anne Calthorpe; she was a lady in waiting for Catharine Parr who was one of Henry viii many wives; in fact, Catharine Parr was his last wife. Anne gave me to Elizabeth I. A few years later, due to misfortunate circumstances, I found myself in an antique shop, until I was bought by a fine young woman named Georgiana Howard and threw her daughter Harriet I found myself in the court of Queen Victoria. Harriet gave me to her friend Harriet Jacobs, a slave in America and through hard work and perseverance, she became a free woman. She was working closely with English nobles and royalty to try and abolish slavery in South America and she went on to write books under the false name of Linda Brent. When Harriet die, I was incredibly sad and withdrew from people for a while; I had seen the true cruelty of slavery and I felt responsible for it. I had seen a side to my imprisoner that I hadn't before and I understood his anger. For a while, my mirror was just a mirror and I hid inside it and did not show my face. During this time I belonged to a woman named Lady Duff Gordon, she took me back to America via the Titanic; she survived and I made my way to New York safely in her coat were sometime later I fell into the hands of a young woman named Helen Fairchild. Helen restored my faith in humanity in me. Helen was an American lady who became a nurse during ww1 and moved to France to work on the front line. After Helen, Sophie Scholl became my owner, she was a German student who seen Adolf Hitler for who he really was, and she protested his views on Jews. The Gestapo executed her along with her brother. I was sold to an antique store by a Gestapo member and there I stayed for 20years until my Annie bought me and moved me here to London where I have remained ever since.'

'Oh wow. You must tell us all about them; we love history. Plus you could be an amazing help with our history homework' beamed Alfie.

'Well, each of my women has their own stories to tell. They have each made their own stamp on history; they have each dealt with a huge historic moment in their own way and of course, with my help. I would love to tell you their stories, but as always I must start from the beginning' Meritamen smiled. The boys made themselves comfortable ready for the story of Queen Twosret of Egypt.

CHAPTER FOUR

'Twosret was the youngest of my siblings. She was a beautiful young lady but fierce. As a child, she was a bit of a brat and very spoilt, but as she grew older, these traits turned into stubbornness and greed for power. She was a very independent person and prided herself on her ability to stand alone. Combine these traits with a very clever mind and you have a dangerous, but brilliant woman. If you managed to get close to Twosrets heart, she could not do enough for you; she loved fiercely but to get close was a challenge that not many people could accomplish. When my father died my brother Merenptah became king however, our nephew Seti believed that the throne belonged to him and so he fought my brother for it. Seti won and became Seti the second. To strengthen his reign, he married my sister Twosret. Seti adored my sister and he ordered her tomb to be built in the Valley of the Kings to honour her. Their relationship was very strong and their love passionate. My sister would sit for hours and tell me how he made her heartbeat race, how she would die for his love. Her cheeks would redden when she spoke of him and it was a joy to see her so happy. Sadly, my sister never bore a child of her own, but she took Seti's son Siptah under her wing and loved him as she would her own flesh and blood. He was a beautiful child and my sister and her husband were fantastic parents. Life was good and uncomplicated. Sadly it did not last; Seti II became ill and died at the tender age of 25. My sister became bitter with her grief and threw what little she had left of her heart into her stepson, the only connection she had left of her beloved. Siptah was a child of ill health, he contracted polio at a young age and when his father died, he was only 10, not the most fitting description for a powerful king. Due to this, he was given a guardian to help him rule until he became of an appropriate age. As Twosret was a woman and not of his blood she could not be her stepson's guardian and so much to her disdain, Siptah was placed under the care of a Chancellor named Bay; who had been a powerful member of Seti II council. My sister despised Bay; he was a cruel man who used her stepson's power in his favour. He built himself a tomb in the Valley of the Kings; his tomb was part of a triad of tombs connected to the ones built for Siptah and my sister. My sister was shocked at his boldness; how dare he give himself such a privilege he was not king and never would be. My sister was infuriated; she made it her mission to bring about Bays downfall. She would take her stepson on walks through the palace grounds and warn him of Bay's plans to overthrow the king. Rumours began to circulate around the palace of Bay's treachery towards the king and his family. Rumours I am sure were started by my sister as she was always very quick to retell them to her stepson. Eventually, Siptahs paranoia became too much for him to handle and he ordered Bays execution. Siptah then assigned my sister as his regent and Twosret helped him rule for the next two years. Until sadly, my poor nephew could no longer fight his illness, he became too weak and died peacefully; sleeping in his mother's arms.'

'Wow' whispered Alfie 'this is crazy I can't believe this really happened.'

'Why don't they ever tell us these cool parts of history in school, instead of just all boring dates and stuff' said Jack.

'Yes, times were very different back then' smiled Meritamen. 'Anyway, are you going to let me finish or are you going to continue to interrupt me'.

'Oh yes sorry carry on' stuttered Alfie feeling bashful.

'When my nephew passed away, my sister became queen. She was a strong ruler and she ruled alone. Many men fought for her affection and she had many proposals, but she could never love a man again like she had loved her husband and the pain of losing her step-son was so strong, she knew she could not become a mother of any kind again out of fear of losing another child. So she sat strong and firm on her throne. Did you know she was the only female Pharaoh to do so? Not even Cleopatra ruled alone, she always sat on her throne next to her brother or her son and they helped her rule. I like to think of my sister as the first feminist. The council's men tried to influence her to either remarry or make herself look more masculine. She decided to do neither, she always wore the most beautiful fabrics and looked flowing and elegant wherever she went, her makeup was always beautiful, and she took great care of her long natural hair. She wore the most stunning jewels and always looked beautiful and feminine. Twosret would always make sure she was carved or painted as such and would never allow the royal artist to have her appear more masculine. I admired her stubbornness and her strength and even now thinking of her; I feel proud that she is my little sister.' A genuinely warm smile spread across Meritamen's face as she thought back fondly. Alfie felt his heart warm as he looked at Meritamen's flushed cheeks she must have loved her sister a lot, he thought.

'Have you ever heard the Egyptian and Greek myths about a man named Troy?' Meritamen asked the two boys.

'Sort of, well I don't know much about it, but I have heard of Troy there is a film about him' replied Alfie.

'Well Paris of Troy came to Egypt with a woman that he said was his wife and he asked my sister if he could pass through the Nile with her, but Twosret was visited by the God's messenger Hermes and he told her to protect the woman, whose name was Helen because Paris of Troy had stolen her off a king from a-nearby land. My sister placed Helen in the temple of Hathor for her safety and Hermes made a ghostly double of her called a KA. The KA was given back to Paris of Troy who sailed home with her, and a great war was fought for Helen. The war latest 10 years just as Hermes had said it would and it ended when the city of Troy was in ruins. When Helen's husband

Menelaus won, he took back what he believed to be his Helen, only it was the ghostly form that Hermes had magically appeared and so once she was won, she faded away. Menelaus was in despair and as he sobbed Hermes came to him and told him to travel to the temple of Hathor, he told him to tell the priestess of the Temple about what had happened and so he did, and my sister reunited Helen and her husband. Or so the myth goes' smiled Meritamen

'That is so cool' said Jack staring at the mirror in awe.

'My sister was a very headstrong woman who proved at every possible opportunity that she was just as good as any man and so when her soldiers went into battle, she would follow them. Sadly, this is how her life came to an end and after a long and sturdy reign, she died on the battlefield. As I mentioned earlier, her late husband had made her a tomb in the Valley of the Kings so there she was placed until her predecessor Ramses II removed her from her tomb, redecorated it for his father and placed my sister in with her enemy, Chancellor Bay. I imagine my sister has had a terribly unhappy afterlife one of which she does not deserve.' Tear's appeared in Meritamen's eyes as she finished her sentence.

'Are you ok?' whispered Alfie 'I know it must be hard for you to talk about these things but thank you for sharing your stories with us.'

'Yeah thanks' agreed Jack.

'Oh, you're very welcome' Meritamen replied. 'Yes, it does hurt me to think back on parts of my past, but I also feel like my stories are important and that they should be told. I believe me being trapped in this mirror, was for a reason and that it is my responsibility to make sure the past is not forgotten. How is mankind supposed to better its future, if it forgets and does not learn from its past? And know thanks to you boys freeing me from that chest, I can continue with what I am supposed to do.' Meritamen looked at the boys and smiled fondly. With their help, she would make sure the women from her past got their stories out to the world, because now more than ever the world needed to hear them.

CHAPTER FIVE

The boys had spent most of the morning in the attic listening to the most amazing stories that had transported them back into an ancient time, but sadly they could not sit there all day. Their mother had shouted them down around noon to unpack their boxes and organise their new room, and that had taken up most of the afternoon.

That evening Rose and Henry went to check how their sons were getting on and decided they deserved a treat for their hard work, and so the whole family put on their jackets and stepped out into the warm night. After a short walk, they arrived at a quaint Italian restaurant. A bell over the door chimed as they stepped inside and an attractive young lady greeted them with a smile, before showing them to a table near a large window. After giving them each a menu and reciting the specials from memory, she strolled off to make them some drinks.

'This place looks lovely, doesn't it?' Mum asked, smiling at the boys as they became mesmerised by the pizza menu.

'Hhmm' mumbled Alfie without taking his eyes off the page. 'They have a spicy Mexican stuffed crust' he exclaimed excitedly.

'Yeah, I'll just have a margarita' shrugged Jack. He wasn't a foody like his brother. Alfie was obsessed with food and had an appetite that awed. Mum would say he had a hole in his stomach because he could eat and eat and never seemed to put on any weight. The young waitress returned with their drinks and asked if they were ready to order.

'I will have the grilled chicken in mushroom sauce please' smiled mum politely

'Steak for me' beamed dad 'medium rare.'

'Can I have the spicy Mexican stuffed crust please' blushed Alfie, refusing to make eye contact with the lovely young lady as she peered down at him threw her thick, long eyelashes.

'Sure, and what about you, sweetie?' she asked as her eyes flicked over to Jack. She brushed a flowing blonde lock of hair out of her face, placed it behind her ear and smiled down at him. Alfie gulped as she did so and diverted his attention to the dessert menu.

'Can I get a cheese and tomato pizza please, and some ketchup' replied Jack.

After they had all placed their orders, the waitress ensured them their food would not be long, before collecting their menus and returning to the kitchen in the back of the restaurant.

'So' said mum once the waitress had left 'how are you both feeling about the house?'

'It's great' beamed Alfie

'I like it. Sure, I wasn't the most enthusiastic about moving' laughed Jack as he thought back on his previous few weeks of tantrums, 'but it grew on me pretty quickly'.

A look of utter relief appeared across their mother's face and her shoulders seemed to relax. Her eyes began to well up and she was thankful at that moment for the restaurants low lighting. She had worried so much about her boys the past few months and part of her had felt resentment towards her husband for taking a job that had meant relocating, but although it was early days she had herself noticed a change in her sons, they seemed happier and she felt that the move had brought them closer together.

'I think we should go to the museum tomorrow' said dad 'what do you guys think?'

'Yes' chorused the two boys excitedly.

Their food arrived quickly just as the waitress had promised and the conversation fell silent as they all indulged themselves.

Dad leaned back into his chair and rubbed his stomach once he had finished his meal as a visual sign that he was full and happy.

'Well that's was delicious' he beamed as he outstretched his arms as if to silently yawn and rested his left arm on the back of Rose's chair. 'How was your chicken sweetheart' he whispered as he leaned over to kiss her on the cheek.

'Amazing' Rose blushed, in response to his affection. She placed her cutlery down onto her empty plate and pushed it slightly away.

'Can we get dessert?' asked Alfie and Jack together.

After the family had finished their meal, they had strolled back to the house, taking in their new neighbourhood as they passed. Dad had told them both to get a good night's sleep as they would be heading to the museum early the next day to try and beat the crowds. The boy's full tummies had helped them doze off quickly. While Jack had dreamt of dinosaurs roaming around the park that they had passed on the way home, Alfie drifted in and out of dreams about ancient Egypt, glorious banquets and visions of a blonde-haired young woman smiling at him through her thick, black eyelashes.

The next morning the two boys leapt out of bed, dressed quickly and raced each other down to the kitchen where mum was stood at the stove finishing off four full English breakfasts. Dad strolled into the kitchen after his early morning walk to purchase the morning's newspaper and the family sat together around the table to eat.

'So what time are we going?' mumbled Jack threw a mouth full of bacon.

Dad peered over his newspaper and laughed.

'As soon as you are both ready'. He took a sip of his coffee and returned to his article.

Alfie was the first to finish his breakfast which was no surprise to anyone. He excused himself from the table and after cleaning his plate, he went upstairs to wash. As he walked across the landing towards the bathroom, his eyes fell on the door to the attic and he thought it best to check on the mirror. He had not seen Meritamen since the previous morning and although he had had every intention of going to say goodnight after the restaurant, he had been too tired when he had arrived home. The door made a loud creak as he pushed it open and stepped into the large attic room. The mirror was propped up against a small stack of books in front of the window just where he had left it. Alfie walked over and sat in front of it. Meritamen's face appeared instantly and she could not hide the joy from her eyes at seeing the young man sat before her. Alfie smiled fondly at her reaction.

'Sorry I didn't come to see you last night' he said apologetically 'I had every intention, but by the time we got home we were so tired'.

'Oh, please do not worry young man. After all, it is not as if I am going anywhere' Meritamen laughed half-heartedly.

'I guess' mumbled Alfie blushing. 'Anyway me and Jack sorted our room out yesterday, we are going out today with mum and dad, but when we get back later we will bring you downstairs and you can tell us some more of your stories. Would you like that?'

'A change of scenery, I would like that very much so' she smiled.

'Ok, great.' Beamed Alfie 'I will see you later then' he said and skipped down the stairs.

It was only a short walk to the museum; when they arrived outside, they stood in awe at the impressive building. Jack thought it looked more like a cross between a palace and a cathedral, than a museum. The building itself was huge; the large wooden doors were framed in an archway and on either side stood two incredibly tall towers. The detail on the building was just as impressive as its stature; there were different stone animals all over the facade like gargoyles. Monkeys, lions even dinosaurs, to name a few. Jack's eyes grew wider and wider with excitement as he took each new detail in. The grounds in which the museum stood was equally impressive, with flowers of every species and colour strategically placed to give their full effect. Now if the outside was dramatic, the inside was simply jaw-dropping, which is exactly what jack's jaw did once they walked into the massive central lobby. A huge dinosaur greeted them as they entered the immense wooden doors and Jack made a beeline straight for it.

'This is Dippy' he screeched while jumping up and down on the spot.

'Well, it's lovely to meet you Dippy' mum exclaimed to the dinosaur jokingly.

'The fossilised skeleton from which Dippy was cast was discovered in Wyoming in 1898' dad read from the small plaque situated near the dinosaur foot.

'Ok, where too first then guys?' he asked while looking around at the many doors and corridors that led off from the lobby in which they stood.

A couple of hours later, the family emerged from the museum's giant doors and back into the sunny, colourful gardens.

'That was possibly the best day of my life' proclaimed Jack, grinning from ear to ear while clutching a stuffed T-Rex soft toy.

'What was your favourite part?' asked Alfie.

'The animatronic T-Rex' stated Jack without hesitation.

'I liked that part too' smiled Alfie. 'My favourite part though, had to be the earthquake simulator and passing through the giant metallic globe on the escalator.'

'Best museum ever!' shouted dad.

'Well, I am glad you all enjoyed yourselves' mum laughed. 'Now who wants burgers?' She asked, which was quickly followed by a loud chorus of "ME's".

Later that night once the boys were ready for bed, they snuck up into the attic and retrieved the mirror. They now sat together on Alfie's bed with the mirror placed between them propped up by a cushion and waited excitedly for the next part of Meritamen's tale. The Egyptian queen's beautiful face came into view and her eyes quickly darted around the boy's sizeable bedroom.

'I remember this room' Meritamen said fondly. 'This was once the sleeping quarters of Charlotte; my Annie's precious daughter. A lovely child' her eyes glazed over as her mind slipped into her memories. 'She had a large four-poster bed in the corner with beautiful pink lace curtains flowing down from it. And, under that window was a cushioned seat that I had sat and watched Annie stitch from hand.' She gave a sigh and turned to smile at the boys, 'but you shall make it your own and it will be just as lovely.'

'Mum said we could go to the store tomorrow, to pick out our wallpaper and get some new curtains,' grinned Jack. 'I want dinosaur wallpaper, but Alfie wants to paint the walls and then put posters up.'

'Well, compromise is what separates us from the animals. Remember that tomorrow while you're out shopping' giggled the queen.

'Can you tell us another story?' Alfie asked.

CHAPTER SIX

The two boys got comfortable in the bed ready to hear the story of the next woman who had come into possession of the mirror. Meritamen cleared her throat for dramatic effect and began.

'As you will remember my last tale had ended when my sister Twosret died in battle. Once she had been laid to rest her belongings that had not been placed in the tomb with her, were split between her closest family members. I was given to a young lady who was a cousin of ours; she had been a close friend of my sisters but did not know about the mirrors "magical qualities" as I like to refer to myself' Meritamen chuckled. 'I was grieving for my sister and so in my depressed state, I did not show myself and chose to reside in a world of darkness for some years. My owner placed me in a draw in her chambers and there I stayed. Then, after what felt like forever, my cousin came to the draw one morning and took out the mirror. She wrapped me in brown paper and gave me to her daughter for her thirteenth birthday. During this ancient time, when a girl became thirteen, she was then considered a woman and eligible for marriage.'

'What?' Jack gasped.

'Sshh!' Snapped Alfie. 'Sorry, ignore him. Carry on.'

Meritamen rolled her eyes and carried on with her story.

'The young lady was called Claudia Procula. She was a sight to behold; an utterly stunning child with long, flowing black hair and large brown eyes and when the sun would kiss her smooth, olive skin it would appear to glow. Everywhere she went, people would stop and stare. I took a liking to Claudia almost instantly; she was kind, funny and charming. When I showed myself to her for the first time, she did not flinch; she would sit for hours and listen to my stories about my life and my sisters. We became great friends. One evening Claudia was called into the great hall of her palace home and was told by her stepfather; Tiberius Caesar that she was betrothed to a man named Pontius Pilot.'

'Betrothed?' asked Jack.

'She was going to marry him' Alfie whispered to his brother. He then turned to Meritamen and asked 'Pontius Pilate? Isn't that the man that sentenced Jesus to death?'

'Yes my child it is' Meritamen sighed; a look of sadness spreading across her face. 'A foolish man' she added. 'Now, where was I, argh yes. Tiberius told Claudia that she was to marry Pontius Pilate. Know at that time Claudia lived in a grand palace in Rome, and although Pontius was a member of the Roman council he was based in Judea and so this meant that Claudia had to leave her home and family, to live with him; something she struggled with for some time. Eventually, she grew to love her husband and her new life and before long she fell pregnant. I was in her chambers the night she gave birth to two healthy, identical twin girls. I have never seen a woman as happy as Claudia was when the midwives put her baby daughters in her arms, Pontius had waited nervously outside her door listening out for the cry that would reassure him that all was well, and once Claudia and the twins were cleaned up, he was allowed to enter and meet his daughters for the first time. It was a magical experience to behold and I felt very privileged to have witnessed it. Labours in them times were known to be very dangerous and it was not uncommon for a woman to die during childbirth, the odds obviously doubled with twins, but Claudia was a natural and all had gone smoothly, much to my relief. A year or so passed and Claudia fell pregnant again, just like before when the time came I was placed near her bed; Pilate waited at the door and we prayed to the gods. This time her labour was difficult; it broke my heart to hear her pain. Pilate sobbed at the door longing to be by his wife's side. After many hours, a boy was born, but due to his difficult entrance into the world, his foot was gravely injured. As he grew, Claudia and Pontius had many physicians come to try and heal their child, but none of them could. He was diagnosed with a clubbed foot, and it made walking difficult for him, especially on the cobbled and uneven streets of Judea. One day Claudia overheard her maids talking about a prophet who had come to the city preaching that he was the son of God. He had apparently performed many miracles, including healing a government officials' son at Capernaum in Galilee. He was called "the great teacher" others called him "Jesus, the son of God". Claudia was intrigued and so that night she came to me and asked for my advice. She wanted to take her son to this man and ask him to heal him, but she was worried because by this time Pontius had become a high commander in the Roman government; he had now taken on the role of the procurator. She did not want to shame her husband by being seen taking her son to a poor preacher, who called himself the son of God. I advised Claudia to watch this man closely; if she could prove the rumours were true and he was a healer, then she should go in disguise and ask him to heal her son. So, the next day, Claudia sent out some servants to go and collect as much information on Jesus as possible. After a week or two, the servants started to return with the most elaborate stories you have ever heard. Apparently, this man had turned water into wine; he had healed the sick, allowed a blind man to see and even raised a man from the dead. He preached about loving your enemies, forgiveness and promised that if you confessed your sins and truly led a moral life, then his father would allow you into his kingdom in the afterlife. This was enough to convince Claudia and so she once again sent the servants out to find out where this man was residing. She disguised herself and her son as poor commoner's and she set off with me hidden in her rags and her child upon her back to find the healer.

We walked for what seemed like hours, dodging in and out of little side streets, passing through crowded market areas. The sun was scorching and beads of sweat ran down Claudia's face as she shuffled along in her dark heavy rags; her son clinging onto her back and weighing her down the entire time. Suddenly we turned a corner and before us was a crowd of people all sat in a large circle and listening to an unimpressive looking man who sat in the centre. Claudia approached the man and asked, "Are you the great teacher?" to which he replied, "That I am child, can I help you?" Claudia then lowered her son down from off her back and told Jesus how he had been plagued all his life by his foot, how she wished he could be a normal child and enjoy running around with his sister's and how she longed for him to live a carefree life. Jesus sat on the ground next to the child and held the foot in his hand, he then simply said: "child you are healed go forth and spread the word of god. Remember this day and live your life in his gratitude". And just like that, the boy stood as if he had never had a problem standing before. Tears poured down Claudia's cheeks and my own I should add. I don't think either of us had ever been that happy, and I who had doubted this man's credibility was in shock and awe.'

'Bloody hell' whispered Jack. 'So, you with your own eyes, have actually seen Jesus perform a miracle?'

Alfie couldn't speak he had not moved an inch the whole time Meritamen had been speaking. It was crazy, but even though her stories were so farfetched, Alfie knew one hundred percent that every single word was utterly true.

'Yes. I have' Meritamen said in a proud tone. 'As absurd as it sounds, yes I have, and I promise you now that young boy walked all the way back home without one complaint and he went on to live a normal, happy, active life.'

'Bloody hell' jack repeated.

'Know as I have guessed you have heard; the story does not end well. Jesus became a hunted man and after his betrayal he was arrested and brought before Pontius; who I should add had not yet found out about his wife's secret excursion, or about how his son miraculously came home one day completely healed and so he never knew about the role Jesus had played in bettering his child's life. Pontius was asked to sentence Jesus for treason, but Claudia begged him to reconsider. The night before Jesus' trial, Claudia had a dream, in which she was visited by an angel of God who had a grave warning. In the dream, the angel showed Claudia billions of people through all of the time chanting, "SUB PUNTIO PILATO" which in translation is basically the billions of Christians who recite in their declaration of faith "under Pontius Pilate he suffered death and was buried". When Claudia awoke, her husband had already left for the trial; she came to me in a panic to ask my advice. I told her that I also had witnessed Jesus' powers and that I did truly believe him to be the son of God, with that in mind I begged Claudia to do whatever she could to save this man and with him her husband, from both their fates. Now, during this period women were, under no circumstances, allowed inside court; in fact, were not allowed to do much of anything until recently in all honesty. So, Claudia had to improvise in order to get her husband's attention. She decided to write him a letter. She franticly scrawled on a piece of paper "Have thou nothing to do with that just man, for I have suffered many things this day in a dream because of him". Claudia then grabbed my mirror and dashed out of the house and ran all the way to the courthouse. Once we arrived, we had to find one of Pilate's servants and beg him to interrupt the trial to hand him the letter. After much persuasion, the servant agreed, and he crept into the courtroom and slipped the note to Pontius. Pontius was known for his temper and so it was a risky move by both Claudia and the servant, but it was a risk they had to take. Once the letter had been handed to Pilate, he stopped the trial and came out to speak to his wife. Claudia told him all about the angel in her dream and finally revealed her secret about how Jesus had healed their son. Pilate sighed and confessed to Claudia how he knew Jesus was innocent but that the public was calling for him to be crucified and that to go against what they wanted completely would mean the end of his career. He promised to do what he could and walked back into the courtroom. Claudia and I were beside ourselves. Personally, I thought and still do that Pontius was a coward; he thought more of his career than he did an innocent man's life, a man that had performed a miracle and healed his son, a man who was quite possibly the son of God. Well, you know how the story goes Pontius returned to the court and tried what he thought was his best to convince the people to let Jesus go, when that failed he offered them a deal; he asked the people to choose between Jesus or a murderer named Barabbas (that was currently imprisoned) to crucify; when the people chose Jesus Pontius announced 'I am innocent of the blood of this just person; see ye to it' and the guards came in and took Jesus away. Claudia stood against a window on the second floor of the building peering out into the grounds below; she removed my mirror from her pocket and held me up so that I could watch with her as Jesus was led out into the streets by the Roman soldiers. Just as they got to the gates, Jesus turned and looking up, he gave Claudia a soft smile, as if to thank her for trying. Tears poured down our cheeks as he was dragged away and out of view. Claudia was furious and she ran downstairs to confront her husband, after a blazing row Pilate crumpled to the floor and sobbed; he knew he had done a terrible thing and he should have done everything within his power to free Jesus. He decided that he should at least give the man a proper burial and protect him in death as he had been unable to do so in life and so he allowed two of Jesus' friends, Joseph of Arimathea and Nicodemus to bury Jesus in a cave tomb. He provided the poor man's mother and some of his female disciples with fine cloths, ointments and oils to clean and wrap his body with and finally, he gave them two of his finest guards to watch over the tomb. This final act of kindness or guilt however you wish to look at it was not enough, however, to mend the heavy heart that Pontius carried with him, after that day he became obsessed with washing his hands and soon the OCD and its origins took over his life and after some time it became unbearable. Claudia became a devote Christian and gave up everything to follow Jesus' disciples, she took it upon herself to carry on the work that he had started and she spent the rest of her life spreading the message of the Lord. Before she left, she gave her valuable jewellery and such items to her children; who I should add were now grown and mature enough to look after themselves, and she sold the rest of her belongings and gave the money to the poor, after many tears and words of love she told me she was giving the mirror to her dear friend and relative Pomponia Graecina. Pomponia was a secret Christian like Claudia and Claudia felt that Pomponia could do with my guidance as she had recently been married off to a noble Roman general who had a vicious reputation. Pomponia had known about me for a long time and we had often sat together with Claudia and had some good chat, so I was glad to be placed in her trusted care. It was an emotional day when Claudia left, but I knew she was going to do what she felt she needed and what she thought to be right. I never heard much about her afterwards except that she died in Rome in Italy at an old age. I assume she was helping Peter set up his church at the time, or it may just be a coincidence that it is in Rome where the Vatican now stands. When she died, she became a saint and her saint's day is October twenty-seventh.'

CHAPTER SEVEN

The two boys sat in silence, allowing the tale to sink in. How lucky they felt to have such a precious and privileged glimpse into the past. Alfie lay back onto his bed, he took a deep sigh and closed his eyes as he replayed in his mind the story that Meritamen had just told him. He had heard the stories of Jesus all his life; his parents were active Christians and had raised him and his brother as Christians too, but he had never really thought of Jesus as a real person, until this point. His heart felt heavy as he thought of Meritamen's words "tears poured down our cheeks as he was dragged away and out of view".

'Do you think he was scared?' he asked.

'Jesus?' replied Meritamen 'no child, I don't think he was.'

'Claudia must have really admired him. I mean to give up all her money and family to finish his work after he had died' said Jack.

'Yes, she really did. He was after all a remarkable man, but my children, the tale does not end there. Are you ready for some more?' asked Meritamen

'Yes' chorused the two boys.

Meritamen smiled and taking a deep breath, she began.

'As I previously told you both Claudia gave me to her relative and dear friend Pomponia for safekeeping. Pomponia was a lovely young lady, her grandmother had been married to Claudia's stepfather and the two women had become close at a young age. Christianity back then was illegal and so Pomponia, who had been converted by Claudia and St Peter himself had to keep her faith a secret. When I came to live with Pomponia, she had recently married Aulus Plautius. Aulus was a brave and powerful man; he was very high up in the Roman army and close to Emperor Claudius. The two were happy and shortly after their marriage, Pomponia gave birth to their firstborn; a son whom they named Aulus after his father. Not long after the birth of their son Aulus was promoted to commander of the Roman army and sent to a distant land called Britannia to secure its invasion. Pomponia could not tolerate being away from her husband and so she begged him to take her with him. We travelled for many days on grand ships and eventually, giant white cliffs came into our view. Pomponia took me out of her cloak and showed me the land she called Britannia. We lived and travelled in luxury, but around us, the Roman soldiers were murdering and torturing the local tribe's people and taking their homes and lands. The Roman soldiers worked their way north securing village after village until they were confronted by "the wild ones". These were a strong and brutal group of tribesmen that the soldiers could not defeat and so a wall was built to separate our lands from theirs. The wall was constructed from the West coast to the East, on the orders of an emperor named Hadrian and so it was dubbed "Hadrian's wall".

Eventually, we settled in a place we called Gloucestershire. Pomponia would go out and mingle amongst the locals and spread the word of the gospel; in secret, obviously, her husband would most likely have executed her if he had known. We lived in Britannia for a couple of years before returning to Rome were Aulus was granted an ovation. Pomponia was an affectionate woman, and she loved fiercely, her best friend and confidante was her cousin Julia. Julia was a clever woman and used her powers of seduction to guarantee herself powerful husbands; something that would later become her downfall, for a while Pomponia had been in Britannia; the emperor had accused Julia of incest and sentenced her to death. She was killed by the sword without receiving a trial. Pomponia was utterly heartbroken and lived the rest of her life in open mourning in defiance to the emperors. Some years later, her son Aulus was by now a young man; unbeknown to his mother had begun an affair with Agrippina, the mother of then Emperor Nero. This evil woman had manipulated Aulus young mind and convinced him to attempt to overthrow Nero and take the throne for himself; he was caught in the act and executed. Pomponia was beside herself; she threw herself into her faith.'

'I don't like this story' whispered Jack. 'I feel sorry for Pomponia she lost so many people that she loved'.

'Yes, she did' sighed Meritamen 'and her life did not get much easier after that either. The council accused her of practicing a foreign superstition, which translates as practicing the catholic faith. This was a way for the council to get rid of her for openly mourning her cousin's death, so she was sent to trial. Luckily the judge in charge of the trial was her own husband Aulus and so he found her not guilty. She continued to actively mourn after that, which caused many arguments within the household, but soon Aulus became ill and Pomponia cared for him until his death. Once he had died Pomponia became much more active in her catholic missionary. She preached the gospel and lived her life with strong catholic morals.

One evening she received news that St Peter and St Paul had been arrested and were being held prisoner in Mamertine prison she came to ask my council on what she should do. I advised her to keep her ear to the ground for any news that may follow, but to not act in a way that may endanger her life. So she sent a messenger to camp near the prison and return once there was news. The messenger came to Pomponia one day at breakfast and informed her that rumours were circulating; apparently, Peter had performed a miracle the previous day and sprung a well in the centre of his cell. This convinced his two wardens Martinian and Processus to convert to Christianity and released Peter and Paul. Emperor Nero was furious and he had ordered the two men's arrest. At this news, Pomponia decided she would visit the men.

She dressed in a disguise and hiding me in her cloak we made our way to the prison. When we arrived, the men had been brutally tortured; they had been beaten with iron rods and scourged with fire for not denouncing Christ. Pomponia wept at their feet and told them she would do what she could to free them, but Martinian told her whatever was to happen to them would be God's will. Pomponia left the prison full of sorrow and we went in search of St Peter to ask for his help. It took many days for us to track him down, but when we did, Peter informed us that the man who had tortured Martinian and Processus had become blind and died three days after the torture had taken place, the man's son had gone to Emperor Nero and demanded the men be executed. The execution was to take place the next day. Pomponia was devastated; it was too late for us to help them. Peter thanked Pomponia for visiting the men and for lifting their spirits in their hour of need. As an expression of his gratitude, he baptised her and gave her the baptismal name of Lucina. Pomponia went to the men's execution and she stood in the crowd, where Martinian and Processus could see her silent tears roll down her cheeks, but the two men smiled at her and kept eye contact till the very end; she was their form of strength. Once the men died Pomponia ordered their bodies be buried in her family cemetery and she gave them an emotional, yet lovely catholic funeral which Peter attended. Before her death she had a tomb made for herself and engraved onto it she had her catholic name of Lucina'.

'She sounded amazing' gasped Alfie in awe 'why have I never heard of her before. It's making me quite angry that history seems to have forgotten all these amazing women'.

'I agree. We should be learning about these women in school' added Jack.

'Well, history has not fully forgotten her; it just knows her as St Lucina now and Catholic's celebrate her on the thirtieth of June every year' replied Meritamen with a smile.

'St Lucina I am sure I have heard of her' yawned Alfie.

Meritamen looked at the young fair-haired boy, his ears had become a very bright shade of red and his eyes appeared to be bloodshot.

'I think it's time you two got some sleep' she giggled. 'No more tales tonight, you must be refreshed for your outing tomorrow. Remember what I told you, compromise is the key.' She added as she faded away back into the darkness of her mirror.

Alfie yawned once again as he carefully placed the mirror inside his bedside draw, and wishing his brother goodnight he tucked himself into his quilt and quickly drifted off into a deep sleep.

The next morning the boys wake to the sound of their mother's voice. She sat, perched on the edge of Jacks bed, smiling when they opened their eyes. 'Good morning lazy bones' I have been calling you two for the past twenty minutes' she giggled.

'Sorry mum' yawned Jack. 'We were up late telling stories.'

'Yeah, sorry' added Alfie.

'It's quite alright boys' said Rose kindly. 'But I do need you both up now, dads got his first day in work today, so we need to wish him luck before he goes'.

The boys climbed out of their beds and put on their dressing gowns, before following their mother down to the kitchen where their father was sat drinking his usual morning coffee.

'Good morning, you lazy monkeys' laughed Henry. Alfie and jack giggled and sat at the table with their father. Their mother had already prepared their breakfast of toast scrambled egg and grilled tomatoes; the smell filled the boy's nostrils and made their stomachs growl.

'Are you excited for your first day at work dad?' asked Alfie as he leaned across the table for the salt.

'well I would much rather be staying home and making dens with you two crazy animals, but unfortunately, someone needs to pay for all this food you consume' their father replied with a laugh as Alfie shovelled a spoon full of eggs into his mouth.

'We can make dens when you get home' squealed Jack with excitement, for he loved making dens nearly as much as he loved dinosaurs.

Henry gulped down the last of his coffee and rose from the table.

'Sure we can make dens when I am home' he smiled at Jack as he kissed the top of his head and turning to his eldest he said 'right Alfie, I am off to work you're the man of the house while I am gone. Do you solemnly swear to protect these walls and those who reside in them?'

'I do' giggled Alfie raising his right hand and placing it over his heart.

'Good boy. I shall be back in time for tea' his father replied and rubbing the top of his head playfully he left the kitchen. Mum followed him out to the front door where she wished him luck and waved him off as he strolled down the street, briefcase in hand.

'Right' said Rose as she returned to the kitchen 'I want you both dressed, washed, teeth brushed and back down here in twenty minutes ready to go shopping'.

Twenty minutes later the boys and their mother stepped outside into the warm June morning.

'Where too first mum?' Alfie asked.

'I was thinking we could go to Winnie's it's a little hardware store just off the main high street. It is also next to a fantastic ice-cream parlour, so if you are both well behaved, you may get a treat afterwards.' Their mother smiled at them kindly.

The high street was busy for a Monday morning. There were hundreds of people pushing past each other from every direction. Jack clung to his mother's hand as tightly as was comfortable. He looked around at all the frantic passing faces and wondered why on earth everyone was in such a rush. He thought about how much he had hated shopping with his mother in their little village in Ludwig but how he would give his favourite toy away now if it meant he could go back there. He missed the smells of the bakery and the noise of the bells above the shop doors as they welcomed in the next customer. He missed Mrs Woods chubby little red face and how she would always greet him with a smile whenever he entered the convenience store. He missed how he knew all the shopper's faces and how none of them was ever too busy to stop and ask how he and his family were doing. This place was loud and angry; there were young mums barging past people with their prams; their babies sleeping threw the event as if it were the norm. Jack could not smell the bakery; all he could smell was the pollution coming out of the back of the hundreds of cars whizzing past them. The cacophony of sounds was deafening; people shouting, cars screeching, traffic lights beeping. Suddenly Rose turned off into a side street and noticed how Jacks grip seemed to ease as they stepped away from the hustle of the main road.

'Are you ok, sweetie?' Rose asked as she bent down to look at her son's anxious face.

'It's very different from the last time we went shopping' Jack replied quietly.

Rose's heart sank as she pulled her youngest son into her chest and hugged him tightly. She lifted him into her arms and carried him down the little side street towards Winnie's Hardware, Alfie following closely beside her.

'Good morning' smiled a kind old lady as they stepped into the store. Winnie was a small woman in her seventies. She had tight grey curls on the top of her head and her face was slim with hundreds of creases in it. Alfie thought she looked like she had been left in a bath for too long. She welcomed them in and asked how she could be of any help.

'The boys have decided to share a room, but they both want different designs' explained their mother.

'Well, this is a tricky one' smiled Winnie from behind her half-moon glasses. 'I think I may have some ideas down this isle here' she continued as she guided them all further into her cluttered shop. She led them down an isle lined with big tubes, sitting on shelves. Inside each tub was a different theme of wall stickers; cowboys, stars, monsters, fish, and dinosaur, Jacks face lit up.

'Compromise is the key' he exclaimed with a laugh. His mother looked at him oddly.

'What do you mean sweetie' she asked.

'I mean we can paint the walls and get these dinosaur stickers for my side of the room and Alfie can have his posters on his side. Compromise' he explained smiling at the look of shock on his mother's face.

'Compromise' Rose repeated.

'Yes, it separates us from the animals' laughed Alfie as his mother blinked in disbelief. Rose was not only shocked by her son's mature approach to the design dilemma but also at the fact that this was possibly the first shopping trip they had ever taken together without causing world war three.

'Very good, very good' beamed Winnie. 'Now, what coloured paint are you both thinking?'

The door to Winnie's Hardware closed gently behind them as they stepped out once more into the sun. After purchasing some wall stickers, a couple of tins of baby blue paint and arranging with Winnies delivery service to have them dropped off at the house later that afternoon, the boys and their mother walked to the ice-cream parlour next door.

'Well, I think you both deserve double cones after that guys. I am so proud of you both.' Rose beamed at her two sons as they stepped into Scoops. Scoops was a large ice-cream parlour but still very quaint, with five little round tables covered with lace tablecloths and each had a vase placed in the middle with a bunch of tulips in. On the right was a fridge filled with different drinks and at the far end of the parlour stood a large glass counter with dozens of tubs, which had every type of ice-cream in that you could imagine. Rose and the boys stood in front of the counter staring at the different flavours for what felt like forever. Finally, they decided on Strawberry cheesecake for Rose, chocolate mint for Jack and cookies and cream for Alfie.

'What cones would you like?' asked the cashier as he pointed out the stand with the five different flavours on.

'Let's sit in and eat them' suggested Rose once they had each received their cones. She was apprehensive about taking her son's back out into the main street and hoped that the longer she put it off, the quieter it may become. It had alarmed her at how anxious the crowds had made Jack feel and the worry that she had previously felt about the move to London came flooding back. They found an empty table and took their seats.

'How is your ice-cream?' she asked.

'It's lovely' replied Jack 'Thanks mum.'

'Yeah, thanks mum' added Alfie.

'Well, you both deserve them. I am very proud of how you both compromised on your bedroom décor' their mother smiled. Alfie took a loud slurp of his cookies and cream.

'Compromise is the key' he mumbled threw his full mouth.

'Yes indeed' replied his mother suspiciously.

When they had all finished their cones, they made their way to the door of scoops.

'Do you want me to carry you till we get off the high street?' Rose whispered to Jack before they stepped outside.

'No, I will be ok. Will you hold my hand tight though?' asked Jack.

'Of course, sweetheart' Rose replied and grabbing both her son's hand's tightly they stepped over the threshold and out into the busy streets of London.

The family arrived home shortly after lunchtime. Jack had been less anxious on the way home, probably because he knew what to expect, thought Rose. The boys had informed their mother that they had some more unpacking to do and had rushed up to their room the second the front door was open. Rose had thought that rather suspicious but chose to take the quiet time to enjoy a cup of tea and read some more of the romance novel she had started a few weeks ago, rather than question them.

The two brothers raced up the staircase and burst into their bedroom. Jack threw himself onto his bed while Alfie took the mirror out of his bedside table draw before joining his brother. They sat next to each other on the bed, the mirror resting on a pillow in the middle of them.

'Meritamen?' they whispered into the glass, suddenly the face of the beautiful Egyptian queen appeared before them.

'Hello children' beamed Meritamen 'How was your morning shopping trip?'

'It was great. We did just what you said, we compromised.' Alfie replied proudly.

'That is fantastic news' smiled the queen. 'And you Jack, did you have a good morning?' she asked kindly, as she had noticed the cheeky glint that normally appeared in his eyes was not there.

'I don't think I like London' replied Jack sadly, tears began to prick his eyes and before he could stop them, they started to pour down his cheeks. 'It's loud and busy, it smells funny and I don't recognise any of the faces' he sobbed. Alfie put his arms around his little brother and held him tight.

'It's ok mate. I know what you mean it is very different from our little village, but it's just a big change at the minute. I promise you will get used to it, we all will.' Alfie tried to reassure him.

'My dear child' replied Meritamen affectionately. 'There was once a wise Greek philosopher named Socrates who once said, "The secret of change is to focus all of your energy, not on fighting the old, but on building the new". I can see in your eyes you miss your old home, but I have been to many places in this world and I can assure you that London is one of my favourites. It is a great city and if you embrace it and allow it into your heart, I promise you it will give you great things.'

'Exactly, look Jack if we had not moved here we would never have met Meritamen and she would still be locked away in that chest. Maybe we were supposed to come here; maybe it's in our fate to be here.'

'That's true' smiled Jack.

'That's better; I can see your spark reappearing' smiled Meritamen. 'Well, now that everyone is happy, would you like another story?'

'Oh yes please' grinned Jack.

CHAPTER EIGHT

'Pomponia died in 83AD at the age of seventy-four; by this time, I was discontented with my existence. I had become very close to my previous two owners and my heart was heavy that I had witnessed their lives come to an end. I no longer wished to exist, so I succumbed to the darkness of my mirror for many years. I was passed from person to person, my mirror is after all very wealthy in its own right and so I was well looked after. I would hear the vague conversations of the people around me and so I had a rough idea of what was happening in the outside world. Eventually from what I gathered the Romans had left Britannia and soon after they were overthrown, and their empire fell around 476 AD. What followed was dubbed "The Dark Ages" and during this time the catholic religion became prolific. I had been passed down the generations until I found myself in possession of a woman named Judith of Flanders and soon out of boredom I started to pay more attention to what was happening around me, although I still did not show myself. Judith was an interesting character though; she was married off at a young age and when her husband died her father sent her to a monastery where she met a man named Baldwin. They eloped much to her families' absolute horror. They had three children, one of which was a son they named Baldwin after his father, this particular child grew into a handsome young man and went on to marry an equally handsome young woman by the name of Elfthryth, who just so happened to be the daughter of the English King known as Alfred the great. He was so such named due to him making peace with the Vikings that had come to reside in England and ended a long-suffering war between them and the native English. So, young Baldwin and Elfthryth wed and she became Elfthryth countess of flounders. The two had a daughter named Matilda and Judith loved this grandchild so much, that she gave my mirror to her as a gift rather than pass me down to her own children.

Matilda was an astonishing young woman, she was incredibly bright and everyone who met her instantly adored her, including myself. For the first time in a long time, I showed myself to her and we became great friends. Matilda married a young man named William, who soon after became king of Normandy and the two had nine children, four of which were boys. One day, William came to his wife while she was pregnant with her eighth child and told her he was going to England to invade it and take it from the current king, Harold Godwin. Matilda was to become Normandy's regent in his absence, a role that she took in her stride for the people loved her. As her husband's battle date approached Matilda became more and more anxious and so, she decided to seek comfort in a chapel she had founded six years previous; Notre dame du pre. She prayed every day for news and finally a messenger arrived with the good news of her husband's achievement the day was the fourteenth of October ten sixty-six.'

'The battle of Hastings' exclaimed Alfie in shock.

'That is correct young man' smiled Meritamen. 'You do know your history. From that day on, Matilda's husband was known as William the conqueror. Now although William had won the throne, he still had to prove to the people of England that he was worthy of it. A lot of his subjects resisted his rule for a long time and he had to constantly stop riots within his constituency, but he had a backup plan; his wife Matilda. Now not only did Matilda have a gift that instantly made people adore her, but she was also a descendant of the English throne via her grandfather, Alfred the great and William knew that the native people would warm to her more easily because of this fact. So, he sent a messenger to Normandy to inform his wife that she must join him in England immediately. Unfortunately, Matilda was heavily pregnant by this time and could not travel, and so we did not arrive in England until ten sixty-eight. Once we finally arrived, we were met with chaos. The English were barbarians; they hated William and refused to live under his rule. William had no control over the country and the whole situation was utterly ridiculous. I informed Matilda of how I had once been a great royal wife and that I could teach her how to make one's subjects submissive. We got to work immediately, by hosting two great balls for all the commanders in charge of each village and town. The first ball was at Winchester and the second at Westminster. Matilda smiled and mingled, she introduced herself to all the important town folk of each constituency and was elegant and polite. The people loved her. My second suggestion was that Matilda should learn the native English language; this was surely to impress the people and that it did. By now most of the villages and towns had come to accept William as there king but just to be sure William ordered that Matilda be crowned queen and she was to rule as his equal. This was the first time in English history that this had ever happened, and the people were confused as they doubted a woman could rule as a king, but Matilda yet again proved herself more than capable. She would preside over court while her husband was indisposed, and she did a fantastic job I should add. The only town that was now still resisting was York and soon a riot broke out that Williams soldiers could not get a handle on. He had no choice but to travel there himself. By now Matilda was heavily pregnant with the couple's ninth and final child and the road to York was long and dangerous with narrow muddy tracks, but I advised Matilda that she try to make the journey with her husband, for if she could deliver her child in York that could strengthen their bond with the city. Unfortunately, the child did not wait until our arrival in York, but he was born just outside of it. To our great joy, however, the plan still worked. The people saw this child as the rightful heir, as he was the only offspring of the couple to be born in England. Even though he had eight older siblings, Matilda controversially encouraged this by leaving him all the cities and towns that she owned within England as his inheritance. The final step to secure the love of the English people came a few years later, when the previous king Edward the confessor's wife; Edith of wessex died, I suggested to Matilda that William should hold a lavish state funeral for the previous king's wife and bury her with her husband as the people had loved him and this act of kindness would soften their hearts to Matilda and her family. So, her body was brought to Westminster where she was buried beside her late husband. The funeral was a grand affair, people lined Westminster's streets and William had an awfully expensive headstone made for the pairs resting place. This final act secured Matilda and Williams's reign over the people and they ruled side by side for many years. Matilda set the tone for future queens, no longer were royal women to be confined to domestication and her successors have been able to play active roles in politics and judicial affairs for the many years that have followed.

Matilda died at an elderly age; she was outlived by her husband who became very depressed once he lost his beloved. I was given to the couple's eldest daughter Cecilia; she was a very religious woman who died a childless spinster. Cecilia was incredibly close to her niece, Empress Matilda, so I was given to her as a gift. Empress Matilda was the daughter of Cecilia's brother, Henry I. She became remarkably close to becoming England's first female king or in other words the first English queen to rule by herself, but sadly it was still very much a man's world at this point. When Empress Matilda became ill, she gave me to her eleven-year-old granddaughter Matilda of England, as she had no daughters of her own. Matilda was a kind child and she loved to listen to my stories, we would sit for hours in her bed chambers and she would be transported into the past threw my tales. Once Matilda was grown she married a man known as Henry the Lion, now this man was very interesting and he had a lot of powerful friends. One Easter in eleven seventy-two he was invited to spend some days in Constantinople with his friends in the Knights Templar. I adored that trip, the men were so intriguing I could talk about them for hours, but I do not want to trail off from the present story at hand.'

'Oh please do' begged Alfie.

'No child, I am telling you the story of my owners and the knights Templar are a story all of their own. I shall leave that tale for another day' Meritamen smiled. 'Now where was I up to, ah yes after Matilda of England passed, I was given to her and Henrys daughter Richenza. Then I was passed on to Marie de coucy; Richenza's daughter she went on to marry Alexander ii of Scotland. The Scottish kings were in a different league than the English. England, Scotland and wales were a very brutal place to live in these years; I assume that is why they are known as the dark ages.

Things carried on like that for a while I was passed from mother to daughter, from aunt to niece, grandmother to granddaughter. Always looked after and cared for. I showed myself to some and stayed hidden away from others, but I was always watching, watching how humanity brutalised each other. I lived in England, Scotland, Normandy, France, and Germany all over Europe really. In

Fourteen thirty-five I was in possession of Queen Joanna ii of Naples when she became terribly ill, so she gave me to her dear friend Katherine de la pole. Katherine soon moved to England with her husband, where she gave birth to her daughter Elizabeth Stapleton. Although not royalty, the family were still very wealthy and powerful, so when Elizabeth was old enough, she was betrothed to a duke named William Calthorpe. The couple had one child whom they called Anne and it is Anne's story that I would like to tell you next.'

CHAPTER NINE

'The dark ages ended with the fall of the catholic church, a terrible era of illness and death known as the black plague and the invention of the printing press. The years that followed are known as the Renaissance; art and literature became immensely popular and people generally wanted to better their minds. There were still many active Catholics within England, but a new religion that had originated from a German monk by the name of Martin Luther called Protestantism, was becoming ever popular. By this point in history, women were looked at as nothing more than heir producers. History had seemed to have forgotten all the powerful and strong women that had passed and now if a woman was too clever or outspoken, she was considered a witch. I had to keep a very low profile, for if I had been discovered by someone whom I could not trust I would have been considered a witchy object and my owner the one who had placed the spell.

I had belonged to Anne Calthorpe for many years, but I did not dare show myself to her until I could fully trust her. I watched as she married Henry Radcliffe the second earl of Sussex and I watched as he divorced her in fifteen fifty-five after accusing her of bigamously marrying Sir Edward Knyvett of Buckingham castle. Now divorce was new to me and apparently quite new to England also. At the time, the king was Henry viii, he was a fat arrogant man who smelt horrific, but from what I believe he was once a handsome young gentleman who had quite a way with the ladies. His first wife Catherine of Aragon had given birth to a baby boy; whom they named Henry, not long after her marriage to the king but unfortunately, the child died just twenty-one days after his birth and Catherine went on to miscarry her next few pregnancies. Finally, she gave birth to a healthy child, but alas, it was a girl. Catherine loved her daughter whom she named Mary, but the king was not happy, he needed a son to succeed his throne. Soon the king's eyes began to wander until they fell upon the attractive young Anne Boleyn, who just so happened to be the maid of honour of his wife, Catherine. Now the rumours go that Henry had tried to persuade Anne to be his mistress and she had declined but continued to outrageously flirt with the king and drive him wild. The king knew the only way to get his hands on Anne was to marry her but how when he was already married. He decided to revamp his beloved Christian religion and adapt it to his own benefit and so the Church of England was born and within this religion, divorce was legal. Obviously, it was not that straight forward and there was much uproar about this decision, but he was king, so he did not care. He divorced his wife Catherine and married Anne Boleyn pretty much straight away in a secret marriage on the fourteenth of November fifteen thirty-two, before formally marrying her in a lavish wedding on the twenty-fifth of January fifteen thirty-three. Within the year, Anne gave birth to a beautiful baby girl whom she called Elizabeth, the king was disappointed, but he prayed that a son would soon follow. Sadly, however, Anne went on to miscarry three times and by march fifteen thirty-six Henry had already set his sights on wife number three: Jane Seymour. To make Jayne his wife Henry had to give a valid reason to end his marriage with Anne and so, he accused the poor women of witchcraft and incest. She was arrested and sent to the tower of London to await trail. Her trial judges were her own uncle Thomas Howard and her former betrothed Henry Percy, the swine's found her guilty and sentenced her to death; she was beheaded four days later. A day after the execution Henry was betrothed to Jayne and in just a few short weeks the pair were wed in the palace of Whitehall (also known as Westminster) and by the following month, she was announced queen. I was quite fond of Jayne as a queen, she was very sympathetic to her people and she showed Princess Mary a lot of affection, which made her ever popular with her subjects. By January, Jayne was pregnant, and Henry waited on her hand and foot. He ordered quail from Flanders and Calais, because apparently that is what she craved throughout her pregnancy, and he ordered that she undertake no engagements for she needed to rest. On the twelfth of October, fifteen thirty-seven at two in the morning, she gave birth to a son in Hampton court palace. Her labour had not been easy; it had lasted two nights and three days. A few days after the birth, it became apparent that Jayne was seriously ill, she died two weeks later. When Jayne died Henry was visibly heartbroken, he wore only black for the next three months and did not remarry for two years. He also organised a grand funeral for Jayne; she was the only one of his wives to actually receive one. Two years after Jayne's death a woman of the name Anne of Cleaves was brought to the king's court as his betrothed, she was not the prettiest of women and apparently, the king could not find her attractive so the marriage was annulled. Now Anne did receive a large sum of money from the king and they did stay close friends and so she was dubbed "the king's sister". While Henry was waiting for his marriage to be annulled, another young woman had caught his eye and that was the lady in waiting to his current wife; Catharine Howard. Catherine was an attractive young lady but with a dangerously flirtatious personality. Not long after she was married to the king, she was accused of adultery and beheaded along with her two alleged lovers, Thomas Culpeper and Francis Dereham.

While all this had been going on, I had been in possession of Anne Calthorpe and had eavesdropped on conversations to find out what was going on in the outside world. Anne had a good friend named Catherine Parr, who was a member of princess Marys household and the two women would often meet up to discuss all the gossip of court. One day a frantic Catherine arrived at Anne's home and informed her that the king had taken a fancy to her. She, however, had begun a relationship with Thomas Seymour, and she had overheard that the king planned on sending Thomas to Brussels to remove him from the picture. Catherine was beside herself, but Anne warned her to accept the king's proposal whether she loved him or not, because the thought of rejecting him was not worth the consequences. Catherine begged Anne to join her at court if the marriage went ahead and Anne agreed. A few short weeks later, Catherine and the king were married and I was placed in a chest with my owner's belongings and taken to my new home in the queen's court.

The Queen's court was in the grand palace of Westminster and although it was not my first stay; for I had stayed in this beautiful building before when Matilda of Flanders had been my owner, I still felt a powerful sense of awe and privilege when I entered through the immense doors. Anne was given her own quarters not far from the queen's privy and she was very well cared for. Catherine was grateful to have her friend close at hand and ensured that all of Anne's needs were catered for. I spent a lot of the time alone on top of a chest of drawers, while Anne attended banquets and balls with the queen and her husband. The idea of showing myself to Anne became more and more tempting and I waited for the perfect moment.

One night Anne came to her chambers and was visibly upset, she had just gotten into an altercation with her estranged husband. She sat at her vanity desk and sobbed into her handkerchief. I knew it was now or never, so I seized the moment and appearing in my mirror, I whispered softly "now my dear don't cry". Anne screamed the place down and darted to the furthest corner of the room. Catherine hearing her friend in distress ran in to see what the commotion was all about. I considered hiding once again, but it was too late Anne had seen me and she stood pointing at my mirror and flapping about like a Nile bird. It was Catherine that picked me up and investigated my face, she was more curious than scared. "How unusual", she said as she turned me around in her hand as if looking for any clues as to how this illusion, she was witnessing was taking place. I explained that I was Queen Meritamen of Egypt and that I had been entrapped in this hand mirror for many years. Anne then became more upset then scared and wanted to know why I had never shown myself to her before. After a long discussion and retelling the story of my life and my entrapment yet again, the two women decided I was not a form of evil witchcraft after all and that I could be trusted. After many hours of talks, Catherine returned to her chambers and Anne and myself were left alone. Neither of us slept that night we talked until the sky turned from pitch black to a blood orange-red and Anne sat against the window and held me up so we could watch the sunrise together.

After that night life became much less dull, Anne would take me on walks around the palaces's grounds and we would sit and watch the boats travelling up and down the river Thames. Catherine; who was still somewhat afraid of her new husband and his fearsome reputation when it came to his previous wives, had started to accompany us on our walks and would often ask my advice on keeping herself in her husband's good graces.

One evening we got word that Henry had become suspicious of his wife and her religious beliefs and had ordered her arrest. Catherine came to me in a panic and confessed she had, in fact, previously argued with her husband over his beliefs. I advised her to brush it off as merely a way to distract her husband from his painful ulcers (Henry had received a terrible leg injury whilst jousting a few years previous, which had now become infected and ulcerous). So, Catherine went to her husband at once to ensured him her playful arguments were just a way to take his mind off his pain, and that surely showed him how much she loved him. Henry accepted this, but one evening whilst he and Catherine were out walking together, a soldier tried to arrest her as Henry had forgotten to inform them that they had reconciled. Catherine thankfully was not arrested, but she was rather shaken, and this event cemented in her mind that her husband could not be trusted; she spent the rest of her marriage walking on eggshells. '

'He was a right horror, wasn't he' said Alfie angrily.

'He certainly was' replied Meritamen. 'Not just to his wives either, his children had a terrible time of it too. He favoured Edward obviously for he was the boy, but the girls were brushed under the carpet and ignored. Jayne had previously tried to mend the bond between Henry and his firstborn Mary, but she had never been able to get Henry to reinstate Mary into the line of succession. Catherine, however, was incredibly close to all three of Henry's children, especially Elizabeth and she was able to convince Henry to pass the third succession act in fifteen forty-three, which would enable the girls a right to the throne, if their brother did not live long enough to produce an heir of his own.'

'How did she manage to get him to do that?' asked Jack.

'Well, Henry was a stubborn, ignorant man and so Catherine had to convince him that he had come up with the idea by himself. She done this by dropping comments over breakfast such as "do you not think it would be a good idea to have a contingency plan dear?" and "Edward will be a great soldier when he is older do you not think. I do worry though, what will happen to the throne if he does not return from the battlefield, and has not had time to produce an heir". Catherine was much cleverer then Henry's previous wives; she was much older than the rest of them and had been married twice before, plus she had me.' Meritamen giggled as she finished her sentence.

'How long were Catherine and Henry married?' Alfie asked.

'Four years dear. When Henry died, he ensured that Catherine received seven thousand pounds a year allowance and she became the guardian of Princess Elizabeth. Not long after the king passed Thomas Seymour; Catherine's previous betrothed, returned to court and continued his wooing of her. They married in secret six months later and when the news of their marriage finally did come to light, it caused a public scandal. Henry's children turned on Catherine, especially Mary and she tried to stop Elizabeth from speaking to her. Catherine was finally married to her true love and she was happy. She fell pregnant for the first time and gave birth to a baby girl, but she was a mature woman and the pregnancy and birth were complicated. She died a few weeks after the labour due to complications during delivery.'

'Aww, that's really sad. She was finally happy. What about Anne, though, what happened to her?' Jack asked.

'Well, Anne had a rough time of it also. As I mentioned earlier, she was accused of bigamously marrying Sir Edmund and thrown out of her husband's home. Luckily for her, she was living within the queen's court at the time, so she was not homeless; she just could not return to the house she shared with her husband. The King accused Anne of practicing what he called "treasonous prophecies", she was arrested and spent five and a half months in the tower of London.'

'What are treasonous prophecies?' asked Jack.

'Well, the king had created his own religion; The Church of England, and so he expected all his subjects to follow that religion. This meant that religions such as Protestantism were illegal and Anne was a protestant; as was his wife Catherine, but she managed to convince the king that she was Church of England.'

'Why did he let his wife off and not Anne then?' Alfie asked confusingly.

'Because' Meritamen replied with a smile, as she was impressed with Alfie for reading between the lines. 'Anne had upset the king. She had claimed that one of Edward the fourth's sons was still alive and this would have meant that Henry did not have a legal claim to the throne. He had to get rid of her before anyone took her claims seriously. Plus, she had been personally named by Anne Askew's interrogators, as one of the women she practiced the religion with. Mrs Askew was a poet and the wife of a nobleman named John

Bulmer, who was arrested and tortured alongside her. Mrs Askew was burnt at the stake after being imprisoned in the tower and for this; she was named a Protestant martyr. Not long after Anne Calthorpe was released the king died. His son Edward became the new King. He was a young boy, nine in fact when he was crowned and he was a protestant.'

'So Protestantism was no longer illegal under his reign?' asked Alfie angrily 'How on earth were people supposed to keep up with what religion they were supposed to be? I can't even keep up with it in this story!'

'That was exactly the problem' Meritamen replied. 'The rules changed that often that the people were beginning to get rather fed up and stopped taking the Royal family seriously, which resulted in a lot of them losing their heads. Once Edward died, at the age of fifteen after a six-year reign, his sister Mary became Queen. Mary was a catholic and went on a bloody rampage beheading anyone who practiced the protestant faith. She was therefore known as Bloody Mary.'

'Another religion' muttered Alfie while rolling his eyes.

'Indeed' replied Meritamen. 'Anne Calthorpe, who was at this time being hunted by her ex-husband Henry Radcliffe, fled England. Henry was actively attempting to pass laws which would not only tarnish her name but would bastardise her children and leave her with nothing. She also feared the new queen might have her beheaded for her faith and so she felt she was better out of sight, out of mind. We fled to France where we lived with friends, but Anne constantly worried about Princess Elizabeth; she knew that she was in danger. Elizabeth was a Protestant and Mary would not care if they were sisters. A hunch that happened to come true; as under Mary's reign, Elizabeth was imprisoned for nearly a year for her beliefs and her sympathy towards protestant rebels. Twice Anne met up with the French ambassador and tried to persuade him to help her sneak Elizabeth to the safety of France, but alas the French did not wish to involve themselves with English politics.

After a few years in hiding, word reached our ears that Princess Elizabeth was being forced into a marriage to the Duke of Savoy and that same year Henry Radcliffe died. Anne decided she could not hide in France much longer and we returned to England to help Elizabeth escape her arranged marriage. On arrival, Anne was arrested and sent to a notorious prison in London called "The Fleet" I was left in Elizabeth's hands.'

'The Tudors were brutal' Jack sighed.

'That they were' agreed Meritamen. 'Queen Mary became ill and she died in November fifteen fifty-eight; her dreams of a catholic England dying with her. Elizabeth was pronounced Queen upon her sister's death and formally crowned the following January. Once again England became a protestant 'Church of England' state.

Under Elizabeth, Anne was freed from prison, but Elizabeth asked if she could keep hold of my mirror, as she may need my council and so she offered Anne a place in her court. Shortly after, Anne met her second husband; Andrew Wyse, who was an Irish Royal officer, and they moved to Ireland.

One evening Elizabeth came to her chambers to ask me for advice. She was becoming increasingly pressured to find a husband, for the men within the government did not feel that a woman could rule without a man. I told Elizabeth of my sister Twosret. I told her how my sister had also felt this pressure and how she had defied those who doubted her and had not only ruled alone but also rode into battle alongside her soldiers. She had always maintained her feminine looks and did not yield when the royal artists tried to paint her as a more masculine character. Elizabeth was so impressed with my sister's strength that she decided to model herself on her and so refused any suitors presented before her. Once when she was questioned by the nobles of when she planned to marry she replied, *"I know I have the body of a weak and feeble woman, but I have the heart and stomach of a king and of a king of England too."*

Elizabeth was a beautiful woman, when I think of an English rose, I think of her. She had long flowing ginger hair, an elegant bone structure and pale skin. She wore the most beautiful gowns and like my sister, she always took great care to make sure she was painted as feminine as she was.

In the early years of Elizabeth's reign, Christians were fearful of Protestants seeking revenge for the actions of Bloody Mary and so they did not trust their new Protestant Queen. The Pope and his Catholic subjects plotted against the queen's downfall and with the help of France decided to attempt to overthrow Elizabeth and crown her Scottish cousin Mary Queen of Scots in her place. Elizabeth received word of the plot (which became known as the Babington Plot) and gave her cousin the opportunity of signing a peace agreement, Mary declined the agreement and instead chose to marry the Earl of Bothwell who had just been accused of murdering Mary's own husband; a marriage that infuriated Elizabeth. Elizabeth decided to arrest her cousin and trial her for treason. Mary was found guilty and later executed. Elizabeth, however, did have a kind heart and after lengthy discussions with her on how the English people must be confused about what religion to follow after the behaviour of her predecessors, she decided to pass the Elizabethan religious settlement; which was an attempt to settle the divide between Catholics and protestants and it addressed the differences in their beliefs. Although this did not entirely resolve the problem, it did make things much better.

Elizabeth's reign is known as the Elizabethan era and the golden ages. The country enjoyed a time were royals, government and religion coincided with each other somewhat peacefully.

Elizabeth accomplished many great things during her time as Queen; her army secured a victory during the Spanish armada and avoided invasion. Elizabeth's friend Frances Drake, a brave explorer, played a major role in the destruction of the Armada fleet and went on to explore South America and brought Elizabeth a potato back from his travels. I remember Elizabeth would always get excited when Drake was due to return from one of his adventures; she enjoyed the unusual gifts he would find and return home for her. Another of Elizabeth's great loves was the theatre and an exceptional play writer named William Shakespeare rose to fame during Elizabeth's reign. One of my favourite memories is of Elizabeth coming to her chambers one morning and excitedly informing me she had a treat for me later that day. After lunch we rode by carriage to a theatre in London called The Globe and there, we watched Williams play Romeo and Juliet; the most romantic love story ever told.' Meritamen sighed happily as her mind engulfed itself in her memories.

'We have done about William Shakespeare in school, he's still really famous now' Jack exclaimed.

'Yeah, loads of his plays have become big Hollywood films' added Alfie.

'Really' gasped Meritamen 'that knowledge fills my heart with joy. He was such a lovely man and extremely talented.'

'So what happened to Queen Elizabeth?' asked Jack eager to hear the end of the story.

'Elizabeth was the queen of England for forty-five years. She had an exceptional reign and England was a happy place to be, where the arts blossomed while she ruled. She never married and so died childless with no direct heir to the throne. She was sixty-nine when she passed after a short illness; I stayed by her side till the very end reciting her poetry while she took her last breath.'

'What poetry did she like?' whispered Alfie as a means to distract Meritamen as tears had begun to fill her eyes.

'All the world's a stage,
And all the men and women merely players;
They have their exits and their entrances,
And one man in his time plays many parts,
His acts being seven ages. At first, the infant,
Mewling and puking in the nurse's arms.
Then the whining schoolboy, with his satchel
And shining morning face, creeping like snail
Unwillingly to school. And then the lover,
Sighing like furnace, with a woeful ballad
Made to his mistress' eyebrow. Then a soldier,
Full of strange oaths and bearded like the pard,
Jealous in honor, sudden and quick in quarrel,
Seeking the bubble reputation
Even in the cannon's mouth. And then the justice,
In fair round belly with good capon lined,
With eyes severe and beard of formal cut,
Full of wise saws and modern instances;
And so he plays his part. The sixth age shifts
Into the lean and slippered pantaloon,
With spectacles on nose and pouch on side;
His youthful hose, well saved, a world too wide
For his shrunk shank, and his big manly voice,
Turning again toward childish treble, pipes
And whistles in his sound. Last scene of all,
That ends this strange eventful history,
Is second childishness and mere oblivion,
Sans teeth, sans eyes, sans taste, sans everything.' Meritamen
sighed as she finished reciting William Shakespeare from memory.

CHAPTER TEN

'What have you two being doing all day?' Rose asked that evening while she and the two boys finished decorating the cupcakes they had made for their father.

'Telling stories,' replied Jack absentmindedly as he squeezed blue buttercream out of a piping bag, trying his best to form a perfect swirl onto the top of his cupcake.

'What kind of stories?' his mother asked again suspiciously.

Alfie sensing his brother's thoughts were elsewhere, suddenly becoming alert to the fact that Jack could possibly slip up and reveal Meritamen's identity, jumped in quickly.

'History stories, I found a book while unpacking I've been reading bits of it to Jack.'

'Oh, what have you been reading about?' His mother replied genuinely interested in the answer as she loved history; and she loved that her sons loved history too.

'We've just been reading about the Tudors.' Jack answered while examining his buttercream swirl before placing it down carefully on the kitchen counter and proudly deciding it was the best buttercream swirl he had ever seen.

'Did you know that Henry the eighth had six wives?' Rose asked as she placed a wafer flower on top of a cupcake before handing one to each of her son's and gesturing for them to do the same.

'Did you know that he beheaded two of them?' Jack answered in a tone that rang with disgust.

'Well aren't you a clever boy' smiled Rose 'Yes he beheaded his second wife Anne Boleyn and His fifth wife, Catherine Howard. Do you know, I think these are the best cupcakes we have ever made! Dad is going to love them, and they are just what he's going to need to cheer him up after a busy day at work.' She added as she placed the last wafer flower onto the final cupcake. Glancing at the clock and taking off her apron, she ushered the boys upstairs to wash as she cleaned away the baking equipment and started dinner.

Not long after the boys had come back down the stairs after racing each other to the bathroom to wash up, they heard their father's key turning in the front door and ran out into the tiled hallway to greet him. Henry opened the door and the sight of his two sons excitedly waiting for him in the hallway, washed away the stress of a busy day.

'Hello' he called pretending he could not see Alfie and Jack standing in front of him 'Oh dear nobody is home…..perhaps I'll go the pub' he added as he pretended to turn and walk away.

'No! We're in look' squealed Jack happily running towards his father and jumping up and down in front of him.

'Oh yes, so you are. Sorry old chap didn't see you there' Henry laughed and dropping his briefcase on the ground, he scooped his youngest son into his arms and held him in a tight bear hug. Turning to Alfie; who was still standing in the middle of the hallway laughing at his brother and father, he said 'I know you're a really old eleven-year-old, but you've still got at least another two years before cuddles are frowned upon you know.' Alfie beamed at his father and ran into his arms.

'Ok guys that's enough. My turn' their mother called, smiling as she walked into the hallway and Henry pulled her into the tangle of arms and legs.

'FAMILY HUG' Jack shouted.

Once Henry had washed and changed out of his work suit, the family sat around the table ooing and aarring at the giant, bubbling pasta bake their mother had just placed in the centre.

'Dig in guys' Rose grinned.

The sound of clanging cutlery filled the room for a while as the family ate in silence, enjoying their meal too much to talk. Jack slurped up a string of cheese that was hanging out of his mouth as Alfie looked on in disgust.

'How was your first day at work dad' Alfie asked as he reached for his second helping of pasta.

'Great' smiled his father 'Jerome has given me a massive office. The view of the Thames from my window is really impressive. I will take you both to work with me one day soon so you can see it.'

'Dad is your office in the big parliament building by Big Ben?' Jack asked.

'It sure is. The Palace of Westminster the building is called.' Replied his father as he shovelled a large fork full of pasta into his mouth.

'Westminster Palace! You work in Westminster Palace?' Jack exclaimed.

'Erm, yes why?' Henry asked a look of confusion etched across his face.

'Oh ignore him' replied Alfie while giving his brother a sharp nudge underneath the table. 'I read him a story today about the Tudors and Henry the eighth used to live in there that's all.'

'Oh yes, your right he did. I had forgotten about that. Yes, well that was in the old building, most of that was destroyed in a fire years ago. The Jewel tower survived though and St Stephens's chapel.'

'Oh you must take us dad, promise?' Jack begged

'I will, I promise. Before the summer holidays have finished' Henry answered with a laugh.

Once they had all had their fill of pasta, Alfie and Jack presented their father with the mountain of cupcakes they had made earlier that day; much to Henry's absolute delight. The boys had then helped their mother with the dishes and cleaned away the table.

'Now I do believe I made a promise this morning before I headed out' Henry smiled 'if I can only think what it was.'

'I know, I know' screamed Jack with excitement 'you said we could build dens' and he darted out the kitchen so fast he appeared to be almost a blur. Alfie, Henry and Rose were left in hysterics as they listened to his bouncy footsteps from the rooms above.

'Go and help him' Rose laughed.

Within minutes the two brothers stood at the foot of the stairs their arms overflowing with blankets and bedsheets. Henry led the way into a large sitting room; the walls were painted a rich green and green velvet curtains hung in the bay window, held up with gold tasselled tie backs. The original wood flooring had been varnished in a mahogany and covering seventy percent of the floor was a massive green and cream Shiraz rug. Two four-seater, brown leather chesterfield couches sat in the centre of the room.

'I call this *the green room*' Henry joked as they stepped inside. They worked tirelessly for over an hour tying bedsheets to the curtain pole, hanging them over couches like a tent, pinning them into the walls and eventually they were done. With couch cushions for walls and most of the room now canopied under old blankets, they called for their mother, who rewarded them with juice and cupcakes to enjoy within the confines of their fortress.

'Can we keep it up until tomorrow? Please mum' Begged Jack once he had been informed it was now bedtime.

'Well, we can hardly go knocking it down now after all that effort.' Henry laughed 'don't worry. I will keep watch while you sleep to make sure no sabotage is committed.'

'I have an even better idea' grinned Alfie 'why don't we sleep in here tonight.'

'Yay, can we mum?' Jack shrieked with excitement.

'That's a great idea' Rose smiled.

The two boys ran up the stairs to their room to put on their pyjamas. Alfie took the hand mirror out of his bedside draw and carefully wrapped it up in his quilt. Jack grabbed their pillows and they returned to the living room. Their mother and father kissed them goodnight and retiring to their own bedroom, leaving the boys alone. Alfie carefully un-wrapped the mirror from his quilt and crawled into the den where he found a flashlight that his father had left for them. They quickly made themselves a bed and snuggled up inside it, placing the mirror in-between them. Meritamen's face appeared in the glass and she scanned her eyes around the den.

'Where are we?' she asked, looking alarmed.

'It's ok. We are inside a den. We made it today with dad' Alfie replied.

'We thought you might like camping out with us in the lounge' Jack grinned.

'Oohh, an adventure' Laughed the Queen.

'Guess what? Our dad has just got a new job and guess where his office is?' asked Jack.

'Where?' replied Meritamen.

'Westminster Palace and he said he will take us there soon and if you would like we can sneak you in our backpacks so you can come with us' said Jack.

'I would like that very much indeed' smiled the queen.

'Great. Can we have another story now please' beamed Jack.

'Of course, where was I up to? Oh yes, Queen Elizabeth, the first had just passed away. As she had no children to pass me down too, I was placed in storage with all her other possessions. James I became king; he was the son of Mary queen of scots. James wife Anne of Denmark found me within Elizabeth's belongings and decided to have me as her own. She had an unhappy marriage and once I had chosen to reveal myself to her, she confided in me a lot about her struggles. James had started as a wise king and a kind husband, but he surrounded himself with ill-advised company and was easily led. He was a protestant and soon he restarted the bloody campaign against Christians. James was a paranoid man and believed that Christians and witches were working together to overthrow him. He wrote a book about Demonology, which he believed would help the general public identify a witch and subsequently bring her to trial. Throughout his reign, he hunted Catholics and witches and many innocent people were slaughtered during this period. Soon people had had enough and a plot to kill the king was uncovered. A group of Catholic men had placed hundreds of gunpowder barrels under parliament and had planned to light it once the king entered the building; ensuring the king and all his parliamentary subjects would die in the blast, but the men were discovered before their plan was completed. Robert Catesby was the leader and the other participants; Thomas Percy, Guy Fawkes, Thomas Bates, Robert Keyes, John Grant, Ambrose Rookwood, Everard Digby and Francis Tresham were all executed.'

'Guy Fawkes? I have heard of him. on the fifth of November, every year we have bonfire night where we set fireworks off and we make a Guy Fawkes out of old clothes and newspaper and then we throw it on the fire' whispered Jack.

'As fun as that sounds, Guy Fawkes is a martyr in my eyes. He was trying to put an end to the persecution of the Catholics. Yes, if he had succeeded, then many men within that building would have died including the king, but in the long run, he would have saved hundreds of innocent men, women and children' Meritamen sighed.

'Why do we remember Fawkes and not Robert Catesby, if Catesby was the mastermind behind the whole thing?' Alfie asked.

'Good question' replied Meritamen 'well I assume it is because, when the plot was uncovered, the king's soldiers went to the tunnels under Westminster and found Fawkes there alone. Robert Catesby and the rest of the plot gang had travelled to the Midlands to try and arouse an army of Catholic rebels. The plan was to travel back to London with their army and secure the city while it was still in a state of shambles after the explosion, but alas Fawkes was discovered before he could light the fuse. So, he was arrested, and Catesby and his men went into hiding in an abandoned house in Staffordshire. They were soon discovered, a gunfight broke out and Catesby and his men were all shot and killed. Fawkes, however, was taken to the tower of London where he was tortured until he confessed the whole plot, he was forced to sign a confession statement and then taken to be hung drawn and quartered in front of the public. Therefore, although it was Robert that imagined the whole idea and brought it to life, it was Fawkes who was front and centre of the public's mind, it was his face on the front of all the papers when the plot was unearthed.'

'That makes sense' said Alfie.

'What about Anne, where was she throughout all of this?' Jack asked.

'Anne, by this point, had enough of her husband and had moved out of their marital home. She moved to Somerset house which she renamed Denmark house. Anne and James had been in a bitter custody battle over their firstborn Prince Henry; James had placed Henry under John Erskine's custody the earl of Mar, and Anne had fought for many years to have her son back. A fight she won eventually but her marriage was in runes by the end of it.

Anne became dreadfully ill in sixteen seventeen and James, who was still her husband; although neither had seen one another for some years, did not come visit his wife as she lay invalid in her bedchamber. After two years of suffering, Anne died. Her dear friend and personal maid, Anna Roos stayed with her till the very end and just before Anne took her final breath she lifted my mirror to her lips, kissed the glass and handed me to Anna.

Anna was heartbroken, she had travelled from Denmark to be Anne's personal maid and she had nothing and no one once the queen passed. King James ordered all of Anne's personal maids to leave Denmark house after her death and so Anna found herself homeless on the streets of England. As a woman, she found it difficult to find work and as I was her only possession other than the clothes on her back, I ordered her to sell me. At first, she refused, but soon she was so hungry and cold she had no other choice. She found an antique dealership in London and sold me to them for ten pounds and ten shilling; which was quite a lot of money back then and probably helped set her up comfortably for a while, but I still feel that she was robbed.'

'How much would that be in our money today?' Jack asked.

'I am not sure about today, young man, but in nineteen sixty it was around one hundred and twenty pounds' Meritamen replied.

'That's awful' gasped Alfie 'your worth well more than that'.

'Yes I felt so too' said Meritamen frowning; the sum still leaving a bad taste in her mouth. 'I stayed in the antique dealers for many years. I stayed deep within the confines of my mirror feeling rather ashamed at where life had brought me, but I knew I had done the right thing for Anna by telling her to sell me and I just hoped that she had used the money to get herself onto her feet. The years passed as did the owners of the Antique dealership. One day, a young woman named Georgiana Dorothy Howard was passing the store and saw me in the window. She bought me there and then for forty pound and twelve shillings.

Georgiana was the firstborn daughter of William Cavendish and Lady Georgiana Spencer. They were a very wealthy and powerful family with a lot of royal connections. Her godparents included her Aunt Dorothy Bentinck (who was the wife of the prime minister), Lord John Cavendish (a politician) and the Prince of Wales who later became George IV. Georgiana herself had married George Howard; the sixth earl of Carlisle and a powerful politician. We lived in Castle Howard in Yorkshire; a massive building that resembled a grand palace than a castle. I remember once seeing a picture of the Taj Mahal and could not help but draw comparisons between the two buildings.

Georgina had been raised by a very hands-on mother who had breastfed her herself rather than hire a wet nurse.'

'What's a wet nurse?' asked Jack.

'A woman who is hired by a noble or royal woman to breastfeed their child for them' explained Meritamen before continuing with her story. 'So, when Georgina moved into her marital home and discovered that her husband's family were more formal with their children, she was not best pleased. I told her to stand her ground and be the woman and the mother she wanted to be. She raised her twelve children in the same values as she herself had been raised by her own mother. Her sister Harriet: also accustomed to a close family relationship, was hands-on with helping Georgiana raise her children. Harriet was by her sister's side holding her hand while she gave birth to each and every one of them; even postponing her own wedding while Georgina gave birth to her second child. Georgina, in return, was there holding Harriet's hand when her turn came. The sisters were inseparable and gave me fond memories of my own relationship with my sister Bintanath.

I was happy in Castle Howard and I enjoyed a good relationship with Georgiana and Harriet; they were fun characters who enjoyed socialising and holding grand balls and lavish feasts. When Georgiana became ill, she gave me to her favourite daughter Harriet; whom she had named after her beloved sister, and when the day came for her to part this world she lay in her bedchamber surrounded by all the people she loved.'

'That's how I want to go' sighed Alfie 'old, in bed surrounded by all my family and friends.'

'I could not think of a better way myself' smiled Meritamen. 'I think it is time you two got some sleep. We shall continue with Georgiana's daughter's story tomorrow. Goodnight' and with that, she was gone.

Alfie turned to Jack only to discover that his little brother was already asleep. The busy day shopping and making cakes and den's had taken it out of him. Alfie wrapped Meritamen's mirror in a spare sheet; that they had not used in the construction of their den and hid her under the couch. In case mum or dad seen her in the morning when they came to wake him and Jack. He would sneak her upstairs tomorrow while he was taking the den down; he thought. Once he was convinced the mirror was well hidden, he crawled back inside the den and snuggled up within the pile of quilts and pillows and drifted off to sleep.

CHAPTER ELEVEN

The two boys were woken the next morning to find their mother and father crawling into their fortress; mum holding a large overflowing plate of butter and strawberry jam on toast and dad holding his usual morning cup of steaming hot coffee in the air, trying not to spill any as he wriggled on his knees under the canopy of sheets.

'Morning campers' Henry beamed at the sight of his two sons. Alfie wiping the sleep from his eyes yawned and smiled at his father.

'Mmmm, toast' grinned Jack sleepily.

'Thought we would have breakfast in here with you two this morning' smiled Rose as she sat cross-legged onto a mound of blankets and placed the plate of toast down onto the floor in front of her 'don't mind if we join you, do you?' she added.

'Not at all' mumbled Jack grabbing a piece of toast and shoving it into his mouth.

'How was your sleep?' Henry asked through a mouthful of toast.

'Slightly uncomfortable' confessed Alfie.

'I slept great' said Jack.

'Didn't come across any wild beasts then?' their father asked jokingly 'no bears popped their head into your tent in the night?'

'No of course not' giggled Jack.

'Oh well that was lucky' exclaimed their father. His face showing no sign of him pretending and the two boys burst into laughter.

'You're crazy you know' laughed Alfie.

'Well, you never know, do you. I suppose it could happen' Henry replied adamantly.

'What a bear invading our den that is in the middle of our living room, in our house, which is in London?' shrieked Jack in-between hysterics of laughter 'There aren't any bears in London.'

'Oh there isn't? What about the London zoo? I bet you five pound that there is a bear in London zoo' Henry replied 'What if one of the bears in London zoo escaped, broke into our house and then stuck its head into your den.'

'Well, then yes I suppose in that case you would be right' laughed Rose as the two boys fell about with tears of laughter rolling down their cheeks.

Once everybody had composed themselves and all the toast had been consumed, the two brothers went up to brush their teeth while Henry got ready for another day of work. Jack rinsed his mouth and left the bathroom. He stopped on the landing outside his father's bedroom door and nocked.

'Come in' Henry called. Jack stepped into his mother and fathers bedroom. It was a large room with a fluffy cream carpet and baby blue walls. One wall was covered in white framed pictures, each picture a different memory; Jacks first bath, Alfie's christening, Henry and Roses wedding day to name just a few. Jack quickly scanned the room until his eyes fell onto his father, who was sat on the large king-size bed in front of the window.

'What's up kiddo?' Henry asked smiling.

'Just wondering dad, can we come to work with you today?' Jack asked quietly.

'Sorry mate, not today. I will check later though while I'm in the office and see what day is going to be the quietest next week and you can come in then.'

'Ok, thanks dad' Jack smiled and skipped out the door.

'What was that about?' Alfie asked as he stood on the landing and watched his brother exit their parent's room.

'I was seeing if we could go to work with dad today, but he said he's going to check later and he will take us next week' explained Jack.

'Don't bug him or he won't take us' snapped Alfie. 'Plus, he might get suspicious if you act too eager. You don't want him or mum to find out about the mirror, do you?' he added with a whisper.

Jacks face drooped as he turned and made his way back downstairs. He didn't like it when Alfie snapped at him. He looked up to his big brother and the thought of disappointing him made him sad. Alfie realised he had upset Jack suddenly felt a sense of guilt knot in his stomach and quickly followed his brother down the stairs.

'I'm sorry Jack' he gulped once he had caught up with him 'I didn't mean to snap.'

'It's ok' mumbled Jack as he disappeared into the living room and crawled inside the den. Alfie followed his brother and sat down next to him. 'Your right, I get too excited and carried away with things.' He sighed.

'You're six you're supposed to get over-excited and carried away, but I shouldn't snap at you. I really am sorry.' Alfie replied as he leaned over and pulled his little brother in for a hug.

'Shall we clean this den away now?' Jack asked.

'I think we better had' smiled Alfie. It only took them ten minutes to gather all the bedsheets into a pile. Alfie reached under the couch and grabbed the mirror, hiding it amongst the rest of the sheets and blankets he rushed up the stairs and quickly snuck it into his bedside draw before gathering the rest of the sheets and placing them into a large ottoman in the corner of the room.

'Boys, dads leaving now' their mother shouted up the stairs. Alfie and Jack darted down the stairs and into their father's arms.

'Have a good day dad' they chorused before Henry kissed them both on the top of their heads and headed off to work.

'What's the plan for today mum' asked Alfie turning to look at his mother.

'Well Winnie delivered the paint for your room yesterday afternoon, so I was wondering if you two wanted to help me paint it?' their mother asked with a smile, already knowing the answer.

'Definitely' Alfie excitedly replied as the three of them ran up the stairs to the bedroom.

Mum fetched the paint, rollers, a giant plastic sheet and some overalls for the three of them and they proceeded to drag the beds, bedside cabinets and ottoman into the centre of the room. Rose placed the plastic sheet onto the floor against the first wall and opened one of the tins of paint.

An hour later, they stood back to admire their masterpiece.

'Good job guys' grinned Rose 'just three more to go.' By lunchtime, they had done the first coat on every wall and the room looked fantastic.

'I think that's enough for now' said Rose.

'Good, I'm starving' Alfie replied. Rose put the lid back onto the paint tin and put their rollers into a bowl of turps while the boys went and washed up.

Fifteen minutes later, Rose called up the stairs that lunch was ready, and the two boys ran down to the kitchen. On the table was a platter of tuna and mayonnaise sandwiches, a bowl of salad, a bowl of crisp and a jug of juice. They sat down and dug in.

'This lunch is great mum; thanks' mumbled Jack threw a mouthful of sandwich.

'You're welcome dear, but don't talk with your mouth full' Rose replied and so they ate the rest of their lunch in silence.

'What do we do now then?' asked Alfie once he had finished eating.

'We need to wait until the walls are completely dry and then apply the second coat' Rose explained.

'So can we go and play for a bit then?' asked Jack.

'Yes of course. I will call you when we are ready to carry on with the painting' Rose smiled as she began to clear the table. Alfie and Jack darted out of the room and ran upstairs.

'We need to get the mirror out of our room' Alfie explained to his little brother 'you stand on the landing and call me if mum comes. I will sneak into our room and get her.'

'Ok' whispered Jack as Alfie disappeared behind the bedroom door emerging second later holding the mirror in his hand. 'Where are we going to go with her?'

'In the garden, the weathers nice come on' replied Alfie as he tiptoed down the stairs. Jack popped his head around the kitchen door, but his mother was not in there. Alfie tiptoed across the hallway and peered through the gap in the living room door. Their mother was lying across one of chesterfield couches completely absorbed into a book.

'Come on we can go' he whispered to Jack and they made a beeline for the back door.

The back garden was huge with a neatly mowed lawn and a border of flowers. At the back stood three overgrown willow trees which curtained off the last ten foot of the garden. Alfie and Jack moved the willow branches to the side and peered through them. In the far right corner was a little wooden house covered in vines. The house's wooden doors were wedged open by the plant and the floor was covered in dead leaves and mud.

'I have an idea' exclaimed Alfie suddenly, passing the mirror to Jack he ran back into the house.

'Where has he gone?' Meritamen asked as she appeared in her mirror.

'Oh hi' smiled Jack. 'I'm not sure. Apparently, he's got an idea' he added with a shrug.

Seconds later Alfie ran back outside, two folded up camping chairs in one hand and a brush in the other.

'Hi Meritamen' he smiled as he approached 'Jack you hold the mirror while I brush the leaves and mud out of here' he said as he began to clean away the dirt to make way for the two chairs. It didn't take long to clear the floor of the house, and once he had finished, he placed the chairs inside and what stood before them was a perfect secret hiding place.

'Cool' smiled Jack as he stepped inside the little house and sat upon one of the chairs.

'This was Charlotte's playhouse' Meritamen smiled fondly as she remembered the hours Charlotte would spend playing in the little wooden house. 'She would bring her teddies in here and have picnics and tea parties with them' the queen added with a laugh.

'I think we should get dad to help us fix it up' Alfie said to his little brother 'all it needs is a clean and a lick of paint.'

'Good idea' smiled Jack.

'I love this part of the garden. It looks like an enchanted forest' Alfie said as he peered out of the door of the little house.

'Did you know that there is an Anderson bomb shelter underneath that middle willow tree?' asked Meritamen.

'What's an Anderson bomb shelter?' Jack replied.

'It is a sort of DIY air-raid shelter. They were made of corrugated iron sheets, that were half-buried underground and then covered with earth, during world war two. A very clever engineer named William Patterson invented the shelters and the government would give a shelter to families who earned less than five pounds per week. Ingenious really, they saved countless lives. This particular shelter was here when my Annie bought the house and instead of removing it, she decided to completely bury it underground.' Meritamen explained.

'Wow. Alfie we have to dig it up, oh please say we can' exclaimed Jack.

'Definitely, but how are we going to explain to mum and dad what we are doing. They will want to know how we know the shelter is there' Alfie replied with a sigh.

'When I am thinking up an idea, I normally distract my mind with something else and then, while I am not thinking about it, the answer will pop into my head' said Meritamen. 'How about I tell you another story to distract your mind and see if it works, she added with a smile.

'Oh yes please' beamed Jack.

'Ok, where was I up to? Oh yes Harriet Sutherland. Harriet married George Granville Sutherland-Leveson-Gower, the second Duke of Sutherland. He was twenty years her senior, but their marriage was passionate and happy, and they had eleven children, four sons and seven daughters. Harriet was a powerful and influential woman, her family was full of powerful politicians, her mother was a rich socialite, and she had an active interest in politics. Harriet had a close friend in W. E. Gladstone later became the prime minister and always lent an ear to Harriet whenever she had an idea or opinion on the current political topics. Her closest friend and ally, however, was Queen Victoria and they had a remarkably close bond. Victoria made Harriet her mistress of the robes upon her accession, which made Harriet the senior lady within her royal household. One evening, Harriet came to me and excitedly informed me that we would be moving into Buckingham Palace to live with the queen and her family.

Three weeks after the queen had been crowned, the day came, we were picked up by horse and carriage and taken to the palace. It was an impressive building, but it needed a lot of work. The palace had never been used before as a family home and, so there were not many bedrooms or space for a nursery. This did not bother the queen too much at the time for she was young and unmarried, but before long she was married to her cousin Albert and the need for a nursery grew more urgent. Victoria and Albert got to work, they commissioned a build for a massive east wing to be added onto the palace which included extra bedrooms on the ground floor and nurseries on the second, as well as a ballroom, galleries and a grand dining room. During the build, Albert ordered a large balcony added onto the front of the palace which would be used for ceremonial events.

'It still is. Whenever there is a royal wedding, the newly married couple kisses on the balcony in front of all the public' Alfie told Meritamen.

'Oh, isn't that lovely, Albert would be pleased about that. Victoria and Albert were very much in love, a love that some may consider obsession. They had nine children and Harriet had her hands full with each and every one of them. Victoria did not enjoy being pregnant and it took her a while to form a motherly bond with her first child, but Harriet was a big help as she had come from a family full of very hands-on mothers.

One afternoon while a pregnant Victoria was out in her carriage with Albert an eighteen-year-old boy named Edward Oxford shot at the queen, luckily the bullets missed but Victoria was very shaken up and it was Harriet who comforted the queen that night. Harriet came to me and told me the queen needed cheering up for she had had a traumatic experience that day. She decided to show Victoria my mirror to help take the queens mind off what had happened. It could have gone horribly wrong, but the queen took it well when she saw my face appear in the glass, she was more curious and intrigued than anything else. A testament to her friendship with Harriet I thinks she trusted her and so knew her friend would not put her in a dangerous situation. Victoria soon realised that having me as a friend could be beneficial for her, for I had many experiences to share and had seen many kings and queens pass before me. We became great friends and the three of us would often sit for hours and have long talks about how politics and the royal families had changed over time.

One evening Victoria and Harriet came to me in a panic and informed me that the prime minister at the time Lord Melbourne (from the Liberal party or Whig); who was a very close friend of Victoria's, had resigned due to a bill on anti-slavery not passing in parliament, the leader of the Tory party Robert peel had stepped forward in his place. As Robert was from a different party (conservative), he did not feel comfortable with Victoria having so many women in her household who had connections with Whigs and so he had ordered her to replace them with women who were connected to his party. I told Victoria to stand her ground, I told her of how I had told Queen Elizabeth to do the same and how she had gone on to be one of the most inspiring queens in England's history. What followed would be known as the Bedchamber Crisis;

Victoria refused to dismiss any of her mistresses, Robert felt that he did not have the support of the queen and decided that he could not form a government. So, he resigned, and Melbourne was reinstated as prime minister. Harriet and Victoria were thrilled that by standing their ground, they had achieved the outcome they had wished for and this gave the queen a new confidence, that she would continue to use throughout her reign. Once the Bedchamber crisis was over, Harriet decided to help Melbourne tackle the issue of slavery. She was appalled that his bill on anti-slavery had not passed in the first place and so she decided to hold lavish dinners in her families stately homes, where she would invite powerful politicians and influential people to talk about the issue with her. She recruited more and more people into her campaign and before long she felt she had a loud enough voice and enough manpower to take on the Americans. She organised a petition against slavery called The Stafford House Address, which was directed at the Christian women of America and had over half a million signatures. It was the biggest anti-slavery petition ever established and sent directly to the white house (gaining a lot of publicity). This was then met by a defence letter by the former first lady Julia Tyler, titled The Women of England vs The Women of America. The context of the reply not only stated a defence against slavery but an attempt to justify the role and lifestyle of southern American women, it infuriated Harriet and soon a transatlantic argument between the two women followed and made the headlines in both countries. One day a letter of support for Harriet was published in the New York Times magazine by a woman named Harriet Jacobs. Miss Jacobs was a former slave, and, in her letter, she had highlighted some of her experiences. Harriet decided to invite Miss Jacobs to England to stay with her at Sutherland House.

The day arrived, Harriet and I were very nervous about meeting Miss Jacobs, we had done some research into her life and she had overcome some truly awful situations but had eventually become a free woman and had even gone on to be published author. Miss Jacobs arrived at Sutherland house around noon, Harriet had set out a glorious English tea complete with scones and cucumber sandwiches and Harriet was very grateful after her long journey. She was a pleasant lady with a good sense of humour and a kind heart. The two women chatted about the English weather and Miss Jacobs trip while we ate and Harriet informed her of some of the events she had planned for the two of them to attend during her stay. I lay on the table next to the sandwich platter and listened from within my mirror. After lunch, the ladies retired to the drawing-room and Harriet picked me up and showed Miss Jacobs the way, Miss Jacobs eyed my mirror curiously as she followed Harriet into the next room. Harriet sat down on a large green fabric armchair in front of the fire and ushered Miss Jacobs into the seat facing her, she placed by mirror down on a small wooden table next to her and called the maid to fetch some lemon tea. Miss Jacobs eyed my mirror curiously again and then turned to Harriet and asked her if she always carried it around with her. Harriet informed her that my mirror was a precious family heirloom and that it gave her comfort, this satisfied Miss Jacobs for the time being and shortly after the maid arrived with the tea and subject was forgotten. Harriet and Miss Jacobs discussed the English government's views on slavery compared to the American governments and how best the English should tackle the situation. Harriet then asked Miss Jacobs if she could explain to her what it was like to be a slave in America; and this is what she said:

'I was lucky growing up, I had a kind mistress named Margaret Horniblow and a mother and father and for a long time, I did not know that I was a slave. I did not know that my mistress owned me. When I was six my mother died and I went to live with Margaret, she was kind to me and taught me how to read, write and sew. As I got older, I discovered that Margaret was my owner and I thought that maybe because she was kind and loved me that she would free me when she died. But alas, when Margaret passed and her will was read, I had been left to her five-year-old niece Mary

Matilda. Mary Matilda was a lovely little girl but her father James Norcom, who was the local doctor, was a mean and vicious man and because Mary was such a young child, he decided that I would be his property until his daughter became of an appropriate age. Master Norcom took a shine to me but not in the ways I wanted him too. His wife became jealous of me and she would give me horrible jobs to do. I soon met a white man named Samuel Sawyer; he was a lawyer and a kind man; we grew close and before long we were lovers. I had two children to Samuel, but as is the law, my children inherited my status and were born into slavery. Samuel repeatedly went to Dr Norcom and tried to buy my children and I off him, but the mean man refused. Dr Norcom became jealous of my relationship with Samuel and he threatened to sell my children to a nearby plantation if I did not stop seeing him, and he would beat me when I refused his advances. My life was hard, but it could have been harder, being a plantation slave was much worse than being a house slave. Plantation masters are evil and the cries of grown men screaming while they are being whipped, is all but too a common sound when your near one of those plantations.'

I remember Harriet sitting in silence for a good while after hearing Miss Jacobs' story, I must admit it was hard to listen too. Harriet promised Miss Jacobs that she would do whatever she could within her power to help the black population in America. During her stay, Miss Jacobs and Harriet attended balls and dinners. Miss Jacobs was introduced to Queen Victoria and her family, to the prime minister and other powerful politicians and other noble men and women who had ensured they would do all they could to help Harriet and Miss Jacobs with their mission. The night before Miss Jacobs was due to return back to North Carolina Harriet came to me with a thought that had been swirling around her head for some days. She thought it best if I went back to America with her guest, she felt that my knowledge and experiences might come in useful for Miss Jacobs in her quest to demolish slavery, and I agreed.

Harriet nocked on Miss Jacobs door, once she was welcomed in she sat on the bed and proceeded to inform Miss Jacobs that the mirror she carried around with her was not just special because it was an heirloom, but also because hundreds of years ago, black magic was used to trap a soul inside the mirror and that soul had become a dear friend to her. Miss Jacobs looked quite taken aback at this point and so I decided to show my face in the mirror. I explained that I was Queen Meritamen of Egypt and that I had been passed down through the ages from powerful owner to powerful owner. I had seen slavery before in Egypt and I was now ashamed to say that my family had owned slaves. I wanted to help her to abolish slavery once and for all and that if she would have me, I wished to travel back to North Carolina with her and help her with her quest. Miss Jacobs agreed and thanked Harriet for allowing me to go with her to her home country.

I had an emotional farewell with Harriet the next day, but Miss Jacobs had promised we would return one day and be reunited. I and Miss Jacobs travelled by horse and carriage to the dock where we boarded a steamship and set sail for the new world.'

CHAPTER TWELVE

'The steamship pulled into Wilmington port North Carolina after a turbulent six days at sea. The year was 1861 and we arrived to find a new president named Abraham Lincoln had become elected. Abraham was a kind and good leader, who was against slavery. Slavery had already been abolished in Washington DC at this point. The south's powers were becoming very unsettled as they feared for the security of their livelihood; vicious racial attacks were breaking out every day and soon a civil war had broken out. The mood was unsettling and although I feared for our safety, I was struck by the fire that seemed to have been lit within Miss Jacobs. We only stayed in Edenton, North Carolina for a few days, once we met up with Miss Jacobs's daughter Louisa we headed off for Washington DC. There the two women worked tirelessly helping former slaves whom had now become refugees of the war. I remember asking Miss Jacobs once why this relief work was so important to her and she replied: "I can smell it, we have a white president fighting for our freedom, and slavery has already been abolished in Washington. If we all stick together, we can see this threw to the end". We stayed in Washington for a couple of years before moving to Virginia were Miss Jacobs and Louisa opened a school that would teach former slaves how to read and write.

After many years of relief work and teaching, Miss Jacobs came to me one evening with a dilemma, she felt that she needed to return to Edenton to campaign for freedom, but she knew it had become a horrifyingly violent place and she feared for her and her daughter's safety. I advised Miss Jacobs to follow her heart, not knowing just how serious the danger was.

When we arrived back in Edenton we discovered that a group of white supremacy's whose plan was to overthrow the Republican state governments in the South had caused the streets of Edenton to become a dangerous place. They called themselves the Ku Klux Klan and its members varied from wealthy and powerful, to poor and common but with one agenda; the purification of American society. These people felt that the white race was far more superior to any other and so that race should be more prominent than any other. They ran around the streets at night dressed in homemade costumes, often colourful robes with hideous masks and conical hats. Their costumes were designed to be terrifying as they assaulted innocent black men and women and burnt down their homes.'

'I thought the KKK wore white robes, masks and hats?' Alfie asked.

'Not at first. The first group wore bright colours; this group was dispersed around eighteen seventy-one once the law clamped down on them. The second group which founded in the south in nineteen fifteen is the group known now for its white costumes. This group was financially funded by selling its members these compulsory white uniforms. The group that terrorised the town of Edenton was the original KKK, a bunch of cowards running round in masks ruining innocent people's lives.

One evening Miss Jacobs and Louisa sat in front of the fire drinking tea and discussing what the next day of campaigning would bring. Suddenly a loud commotion was heard from outside, Miss Jacobs and Louisa ran to the window to see what was going on. I heard Louisa give out a shriek before Miss Jacobs walked over to the dresser were my mirror had been placed and carefully picked me up. "Meritamen you need to see this" she whispered, I could hear the pain in her voice as she walked me over to the window and pulling the netting gently to one side, she pressed me up against the glass. The scene that was playing out before my very eyes was excruciating to watch. I had seen the young man before; he was a freed slave and was trying to set himself up a little business doing gardening. He was a handsome man and a hard worker; he would come to Miss Jacobs once a week and mow the lawn before going off and tidying up the other gardens in the village. "Miss Jacobs, I swear you do make the best ice-cold lemonade in the whole of North Carolina" he would smile at her as she offered him a glass.

The young man that was before my eyes know was unrecognisable; he laid crumpled up in a ball on the street, five men in colourful robes and hideous masks attacking him. Behind them a house was in flames I recognised it instantly as the young man's mother's house. Miss Jacobs sobbed powerless to do anything but watch on in horror. I asked her to turn me around, so I did not have to watch anymore, but she replied "no, you have to watch this. When we are all dead and gone, you're all that is going to be left. You have to watch and then you make sure nothing like this ever happens again. Do you hear me?" Tears poured down my cheeks as I forced myself to watch; my eyes burning because I refused to blink and suddenly it was over. The young gardener lay lifeless on the ground the five cowards in masks skulking off down the street to find their next victim. Louisa fell to the floor in fits of sobs, but Miss Jacobs stood glued to the spot staring out into the night.

The next morning it was decided that Edenton was too dangerous a place to stay. Last night it was the young gardener and his mother, but the next night it could be us, there were no reasons for these attacks and the longer we stayed, the more we tempted our fate. I managed to persuade Miss Jacobs and Louisa to travel back to England. We would write a letter to Harriet before we left to let her know we were returning. Miss Jacobs was worried that we would arrive before the letter, but I assured her as long as she was with me there would be no offence caused. And so Miss Jacobs and Louisa packed up their belongings and the next afternoon we made our way back to Wilmington Port to board the steamship to England.'

'Boys, boys, where are you?' Rose's voice called from the house.

'Here mum. Coming' replied Alfie.

'That story was horrible' whispered Jack whipping tears from his eyes 'I really didn't like that'.

'I only tell of the truth' Meritamen replied. 'There are many dark times throughout history but only by speaking of them do we give them the hope of light'.

'We better go to mum' Alfie whispered to his brother as he carefully tucked the mirror into his jacket pocket.

Rose had called the two boys in to help her finish the second coating of their bedroom and it had not taken her long to realise that there was something the matter with her two sons who were both uncharacteristically quite.

'Ok what is it?' she asked.

'We have been reading that history book again and it just had us talking. Why are there so many horrible times in the past. I don't understand why humans are such evil creatures' Alfie exclaimed.

'What are you talking about sweetie?' Rose asked, slightly alarmed.

'Well there's all the killing over people's religion and the king cutting off his wives heads during the Tudor times, then there's the witch hunts and then slavery. Why is it always about humans hurting each other? We're all the same, we're all human with one heart and one brain. We all bleed when we were cut. Were all born and we all die. Why can't we just be nice?' Alfie frustratingly asked.

Rose smiled sweetly at her oldest son as she dropped her paintbrush back into the pot and pulled him in for a hug.

'I am pretty sure you're not the first to ask them questions and you certainly won't be the last. As much as I would love to be able to stand here now and tell you that I have the answers, I'm afraid I don't. All I can tell you is that they are the right questions to ask and I am so proud that you asked them. If more and more people think like you and ask these questions, then maybe one day we might not need to ask them anymore. But for now, keep reading them history books because the worst mistake us as humans could ever make is to forget our past.' She kissed the top of her sons head and returned to her paintbrush.

Alfie and Jack stood over the bathroom sink, watching the warm water wash away the blue paint from their hands.

'You know I had a cob on with her?' Jack whispered.

'So did I' Alfie replied.

'I haven't now though. Meritamen has been around for hundreds and hundreds of years; most of her stories are going to be horrible because some parts of history are horrible. She wasn't doing anything wrong by telling us; she was just telling us the truth' added Jack.

'Mum was right. Its Meritamen's responsibility to tell us what she's seen and we shouldn't make her feel bad about that. Come on, let's go and get her' Alfie said as he dried his hands and led the way out the bathroom.

The two boys snuck down the stairs to the cloak cupboard by the back door of the house. Alfie leaned in and rooted around in the back until his hands fell upon a large lump which was his coat rolled up into a ball. He pulled it out and unravelled it to reveal the mirror.

'Well I must say it is awfully dusty in there' spat Meritamen once she had been uncovered.

'Sorry' replied Alfie bashfully.

'And I'm sorry I got upset with you' added Jack 'It just wasn't a nice story, but I know that isn't your fault, like you said you're only telling us the truth'.

'Yes well, maybe I need to remind myself that you are only young boys and perhaps some stories should be censored or completely diverted' Meritamen snarled.

'Oh no, please don't do that. You need to tell us it's, your job to I get that now' Alfie burst out.

'Very well, but later. I wish to collect my thoughts. Whatever you do, do not put me back in that dusty cupboard' and with that, she was gone.

Alfie turned and looked at his brother 'I think she is upset with us' he sighed.

'You think!' Jack replied as he rolled his eyes. The two boys strolled back up the stairs to their bedroom. Jack waited outside while Alfie carefully entered the room and returned the mirror back to his bedside table.

'Our room looks really good' Alfie smiled as he remerged from the room.

'I hope it's dry before dad comes home. I can't wait to show him it all finished with our posters up' smiled Jack.

'Do you think she is going to speak to us again?' Alfie wondered.

'I hope so, but I think we just need to give her some space for now' Jack replied.

Later that afternoon the boys and their mother returned all of the bedroom furniture back to its rightful place and decorated the room with dinosaur stickers and computer game posters.

'Happy?' Rose asked her son's as they stood back to examine their finished work.

'Very' smiled Alfie.

'I love it' beamed Jack. Just then, the front door downstairs closed.

'Daddy' cried Jack.

'Hello darling we're up here' shouted Rose as she popped her head around the door into the landing. Seconds later, Henrys smiling face entered the room.

'Well haven't you three been busy today' he beamed as he scanned the newly decorated room 'well-done guys you have done an amazing job.'

'Thanks dad we are really happy with it' smiled Alfie.

'I think you all deserve a treat. Be ready in half an hour' their father smiled as he left the room to shower and change.

CHAPTER THIRTEEN

'Where are we going?' Rose asked suspiciously as Henry stopped the car at a red light.

'I told you it is a surprise' he smiled. Alfie and Jack both peered out of the back windows of their father's jeep. They watched as the shop owners locked up their businesses, pulled down the shutters and got into their cars to head home after another busy day on the London high street. The red light flicked to green and their father turned left onto a long road lined with designer shops. They carried on driving for twenty minutes or so and suddenly the car stopped.

'We're here' Henry said as he turned and smiled at his two sons. Jack jumped out of the car and looked around. They were parked in a large carpark right next to the River Thames. Across the river stood a large building lined with hundreds of windows. Jacks eyes followed the long building until they fell onto a tall tower he followed the tower up until his eyes met the face of a huge clock.

'Is that Big Ben' he gasped.

'It sure is' smiled Henry. 'Would you like a better view?'

Jack turned and looked at his father who was pointing at the biggest Ferris wheel Jack and Alfie had ever seen.

'Wow' gasped the two boys.

'Oh Henry' beamed Rose 'What a treat!'

The family paid for their tickets at the Millennium wheel box office and then stepped inside the ridiculously large glass pod that they were assigned. The electric doors closed behind them and Alfie and Jack sat on the floor of the pod leaning against the glass while Henry and Rose made themselves comfortable on the leather seats positioned in the middle of the pod. Jack squealed as the wheel gave a slight jolt and began to turn. The sun was beginning to set over the Thames and London was lit up with what looked like hundreds and thousands of fairy lights. They rose higher and higher before stopping for a couple of minutes at the very top of the wheel.

'London looks so pretty from up here' Alfie smiled.

'It's beautiful. We are as high as Big Ben now look' beamed Jack excitedly.

'I wish Meritamen could see this' Alfie whispered to his brother.

'Maybe she can' Jack smiled before turning to his mother 'mum can I lend your phone to take a photo?' he asked.

'Good idea' whispered Alfie.

****

'That was so much fun' exclaimed Jack as they stepped out of their pod.

'Yeah it was great. Thanks dad.' Alfie beamed.

'You're very welcome' smiled Henry. 'You guys hungry?'

'Starving' the two brothers replied.

Henry guided them across the road and after a short walk down a narrow street, they found a very authentic-looking, little Mexican restaurant. The smell of fresh bread, grilled chicken and spices hit them as they walked inside and was greeted by a smiling, middle-aged man who introduced himself as Mario. Mario showed them to a table in the far corner of the restaurant and took their drink orders, before hurrying threw a swinging door at the other end of the room and proceeded to shout at someone named Marcus. Jack and Alfie giggled and buried their faces into the menu.

'He's the boss' explained Henry 'I came here for a work meeting yesterday the foods delicious. Mario has run this place with his family for the past thirty years. He told me that most of the recipes had been passed down from his grandmother and Marcus is his youngest son who he is training up as a chef, but he keeps getting things wrong'.

Mario soon returned with their drinks and grinned at Henry as he recognised him from the previous day.

'Hello I know you' he beamed. 'Back so soon? My grand mamma's recipes have been known to be addictive' he joked.

'Yes I thought I would show my family the secret gem I had discovered' smiled Henry.

'Very good, Very good.' Mario beamed. 'What can I get you?'

'Can we get three plates of Fajitas, two chicken, one steak. A portion of potato wedges and a portion of rice please'.

The sun had completely set by the time they had finished their meal and made their way back home. The roads were a lot quieter and the journey home was shorter than it had been earlier.

'Thank you for a lovely night' gushed Rose as she leaned over and kissed Henry's cheek once they had pulled up outside their house.

'You're very welcome' Henry replied.

Once the two boys were washed and in their pyjamas, their parents came up to their room to tuck them into their beds.

'Try to get a good night's sleep tonight boys' their father whispered as he kissed their heads 'I am taking you both to work with me in the morning.' He grinned as he stood and left the room.

Alfie and Jack waited until their parent's footsteps were out of earshot before they retrieved the mirror from its hiding place in the small wooden draw of the bedside cabinet. They both then jumped onto Alfie's bed before whispering the Egyptian queen's name into the glass.

'Hello boys' Meritamen smiled as her face appeared in the mirror.

'Hi Meritamen' beamed Jack 'can we be friends again now?' he asked.

'Of course' she replied.

'Good. We have so much to tell you' Alfie grinned before proceeding to fill Meritamen in on the night's adventures.

'This magical wheel you speak of sounds wonderful' gasped the queen.

'It's not magical' Jack giggled. 'It's powered by electricity, although the view is pretty magical.'

'We took a photo for you with our mum's phone, but she has gone to bed now so I will have to show you it tomorrow' explained Alfie.

'Phone? You mean a telephone? How can you possibly take a photograph with a telephone' Meritamen asked confusingly.

'We will show you tomorrow' Alfie answered in between bursts of laughter.

'Want to hear the best bit?' asked Jack. 'Dad's taking us to Westminster Palace in the morning' he blurted before Meritamen had time to answer.

'And we are taking you with us' added Alfie.

'Oh, my goodness, how fantastic' the Queen exclaimed. 'Well, in that case, my princes we must have a night of glorious rest. I wish to be fresh for our excursion. Goodnight'. And just like that, she was gone.

'As disappointed as I am that she hasn't told us another story, I have to say she's right. I am exhausted' Alfie said as he turned to see his brother's disheartened face.

'Yes so am I actually' Jack replied with a yawn. Alfie returned the mirror back to the draw and Jack jumped into his own bed. The two brothers wished each other goodnight and fell quickly into a deep sleep.

CHAPTER FOURTEEN

'Wake up, wake up!' shouted Jack as he proceeded to jump up and down on his brother's bed. It was six am, but Jack was too excited to sleep any longer. He jumped down off the bed and opened the draw to the bedside cabinet.

'Meritamen wake up' he grinned. 'It's morning, today's the day.'

'Good morning' beamed Meritamen as she appeared into the glass. 'What's the plan for today then? How are we to sneak me out of this house?' she asked.

'I have a plan'. Yawned Alfie as he opened his eyes and took a long stretch. He made his way across the room to a large wooden wardrobe in the far corner and pulled an old rucksack out from inside it. 'This is my old school bag it has a rip in it right here, see?' He asked as he stuck his index finger, threw a hole in the centre of the bag. 'I can put you in here with some other things so that you stay upright and you can look through the hole as we walk around.'

'What a splendid idea, you clever boy' the Queen grinned.

Alfie and Jack placed the mirror into the bag and filled the rest of the space with some t-shirts and a towel to ensure the mirror would stay upright. They then checked to make sure the hole was wide enough for the queen to see out of and once they were happy, they placed the bag onto Alfie's bed before going downstairs for their breakfast.

Their mother was sat in her dressing gown at the dining table, sipping a cup of tea. She smiled at the boys as they entered the kitchen.

'You two are up early'.

'We are going to work with dad today. Where is he?' Jack asked as he scanned the room, looking for his father.

'Don't worry. He is upstairs getting changed. Would you like some breakfast?' Rose asked as she stood and walked across the kitchen to put on some toast.

'Morning campers' Henry smiled as he entered the kitchen. 'You two ready for a busy day in the office?'

'Oh yes we are!' giggled Jack.

'I have made you each a packed lunch for today' smiled Rose as she held up three brown paper bags.

'What are you going to do with yourself today, mama bear?' Henry asked as he leaned towards Rose and kissed her cheek.

'I am going to have a nice bath and do some interview preparation' she replied.

'Sounds wonderful, good luck' her husband replied affectionately before turning to his sons and exclaiming in a mock army sergeant voice. 'We are leaving this abode at zero eight hundred hours. I need you washed, dressed and ready for action in thirty minutes.'

The two boys sprang from the table and darted up the stairs.

Thirty minutes later, Alfie and Jack climbed into the back of their father's jeep, while Alfie clung onto his old battered rucksack as if his life depended on the safety of its contents.

'Why have you brought that old thing?' His father asked while eyeing the bag suspiciously.

'It has our lunches in' answered Alfie trying to sound as a matter of fact as he possibly could.

'Hmm, that explains it' laughed Henry as he indicated the car and pulled out into the street.

The roads were excruciatingly busy and the drive to Westminster Palace took over an hour, but for the two excited boys in the back of the jeep, it felt like a century.

'This is exactly why I normally get the tube into work' their father exclaimed as he slammed on for the second time to avoid a black hackney which had just pulled out right in front of them.

'You lot don't own the bloody roads you know' Henry screamed out the window at the driver.

Finally, they arrived at the parliament building and their father showed his work badge to a security guard who raised a barrier so they could enter the car park. Henry pulled the car into a reserved space with a little plaque attached to the wall with his name on.

'This parking space is reserved for Henry Asheton' Jack read as he squinted at the sign 'wow dad you have your own parking space that is so cool' he exclaimed.

'I sure do kiddo' giggled Henry. 'You two ready?' He asked. 'Ok, follow me.' And taking his sons by the hand, he led them to the main entrance of Westminster palace. They walked past a huge archway with an immense wooden door inside it. The archway stood at the base of a long tower.

'Is that the entrance?' Gasped Jack.

'No, well yes, it is *an* entrance, but that is called the sovereign's entrance. That is where the queen enters when she comes here and that tower is called Victoria tower after Queen Victoria. There she is, do you see?' Their father asked as he pointed up to a stone sculpture which decorated the entrance to the archway.

'Cool' whispered Alfie as they walked past.

'We enter just around this corner' their father exclaimed 'This tower is called St Stephens tower and at its base is the public entrance. Here we go, boys, stay close now ok.' Henry led the boys threw the large wooden doors and into a grand hall lined with benches and huge paintings. 'Right I will take you to my office first and then we can pop along and have a nose at some of the other parts of the building. Sound good?'

'Yes, sounds great. Are we allowed to go and see big ben?' asked Jack.

'Even better, you are allowed *inside* Big Ben. How does that sound?' His father grinned.

Henry led his sons up a grand staircase and along long corridors. Finally, they arrived at an old wooden door which Henry opened to reveal a very spacious office. A large wooden desk sat directly opposite the door and behind it were two large windows which gave the most spectacular view over the River Thames. On the far right wall was an impressive open flame fire, framed with a large marble fireplace and next to it stood a tall bookshelf rammed with old political texts.

'This office is really great dad. I'm really proud of you' Alfie smiled at his father once he had taken it all in.

'Cheers buddy' Henry blushed. Suddenly there came a knock on the office door, which slowly opened to reveal a man stood in the doorway.

'Sorry to interrupt' the man apologised. He was a slim man with a kind face. He had short white hair and a scruffy white beard. He was wearing an old navy suit with a clean white shirt and a red tie and his brown leather shoes made a clopping sound on the wooden floor as he entered the room. 'Just a quick one Henry, do you have the paperwork on you for Nigel?'

'I certainly do Jerome' Henry grinned at the man as he walked around his desk and opened a drawer. Taking out a small stack of papers he handed them to Jerome and gesturing to the two boys he said 'Jerome I would like to introduce you to my sons, Alfie and Jack. Boys this is Jerome Calvin, my boss'.

'Wow you're the prime minister aren't you' exclaimed Alfie excitedly.

'I certainly am yes young man. It is a pleasure to meet you both. I have been informed that you two are very interested in History. Did you know that this building is one of the oldest in London? It was built in ten sixteen and used to be the home for the royal family, but sadly a fire in eighteen thirty-four demolished most of it. It was rebuilt in eighteen forty, but there are still a few of the medieval structures that survived. For example, parts of St Stephen's tower where you entered, Westminster hall, parts of St Mary's chapel and the jewel tower. Would you like a tour?' The prime minister grinned.

'Oh yes please' beamed Jack.

'Fantastic' smiled Jerome as he leaned over Henry's office desk and picking up the phone he pressed only one number on the telephone keypad 'Mary! Hello Mary, could you cancel all my appointments between now and lunch please? I am giving a tour. Thank you that is all' he exclaimed before slamming the telephone back down into its holder and turning towards the door.

'Sir, is that wise?' Henry called after him 'I can take the boys'

'Nonsense Henry, you're new here, you would be an awful tour guide' Jerome exclaimed before Henry could even finish his sentence. 'Now come on boys hurry along firstly we shall venture into Victoria tower.' The two boys giggled and sped up their walking pace to keep up with the prime minister, who was clearly very excited to be given a distraction from his day's work.

After a short walk, the boys found themselves stood at the foot of a humungous spiral staircase.

'Do we have to climb up that?' gasped Jack.

'We certainly do. It isn't as bad as it looks.' laughed Jerome 'Only fourteen floors high' he added as he started to march up the steps. 'Twelve of the floors are used for archives' he explained as the boys and their father climbed the steps behind him. 'And if you look out of the stain glass windows on your way up the views over London just get better and better.'

As they reached the second floor of the tower, Jerome stopped and ushered them through a heavy wooden door.

'This is the first floor of the archives. We have documents in here dating back to fourteen ninety-seven.' He told them as he led them down a long row of shelves. The shelves were packed with hundreds of rolls of parchment. Jerome carefully pulled one down and unravelled it to reveal a very old banner. 'This banner was taken off two suffragettes named Muriel Matters and Helen Fox. They chained themselves to the ladies gallery in the chamber of commons. To this day padlocks are banned from the building' he giggled as he placed the banner back upon its shelf. 'Exceptional women the suffragettes do you know much about them?'

'They protested for women's votes' said Alfie.

'Yes they did young man. Very brave women' smiled Jerome as he scanned the shelves for another document of interest. 'Arrhh here we are. Take a look at this one' he said as he pulled out another very old roll of parchment and unravelled it onto a nearby wooden table. The two boys and their father crowded round as Jerome read aloud the context of the document.

'The whole number of slaves taken on board on the coast were eighty-one male, forty-four female above four feet four inches. Fourteen male, eight female under four feet four inches. Arrived at St Vincent the fourth day of October seventeen ninety-three.' He read. 'This document is a certificate of slaves taken on board 'The Express' which was a slave ship. It goes on to state how many slaves survived the journey and actually arrived at the port, but I shan't read that part. However, this document is very important as it was used as evidence to help pass the abolition of slavery bill.' Jerome glanced at the boys as he placed the certificate back onto its shelf. 'Not all history is nice' he whispered at their sullen faces before turning back to search the shelves. 'Here we go' he grinned as he very gently removed another very old roll of parchment off of the shelf and again unravelled it onto the nearby table. 'Now this is actually a petition to the House of Lords off Archbishop Lawd, he was being held prisoner at the Tower of London in sixteen fourteen and it reads "for a buttler and cook, without which he knows how to live". So this shows us that the towers living conditions were not suitable for an upper-class citizen such as the archbishop.' Jerome laughed as he returned the parchment back to its home on the shelf.

'Did he ever receive them?' asked jack 'a cook and butler?'

'I highly doubt it.' Jerome laughed as he led the boys and their father back down the spiral staircase.

'Are we not going to the top?' Alfie asked

'Not today there is much more to see and I don't want to kill your poor father' Jerome said flashing a smile at Henry who had been very out of breath when they had first arrived in the archive room.

'Wise move sir' laughed Henry.

Jerome told the boys some facts about the tower as they proceeded down the staircase.

'Victoria Tower was once the tallest tower in the world standing at a huge three hundred and twenty-five feet. The gateway of the tower was built wide enough so that the queen can ride through in her coach on ceremonial days.' Soon they arrived back at the bottom of the stairs and Jerome led them through a door which led to yet another flight of stairs. 'This staircase is called "the sovereigns staircase" it leads to The Norman Porch. It is the processional route the Queen takes when she is to enter parliament.' Jerome explained as they ascended the staircase.

'Why is it called The Norman Porch? 'Alfie asked.

'Because it was originally built to house statues of the Norman Kings' Jerome explained as he led them into the large room. 'Now if you follow me into this room. This is called the Robing Room. The queen will enter this room and put on the imperial crown and robes before making her way to the House of Lords.' Jerome led them into a large room with blue carpet and a gold ceiling. The walls were covered with large paintings and stained glass windows. On the far left of the room was a red altar with a large lavish, gold throne sat upon it and adjacent to that was a massive gold and marble fireplace. Alfie and Jack stood in the centre of the room trying to take it all in; it really was a room fit for a king or queen. Jerome continued his tour through lavishly designed rooms, the gold ceilings, giant paintings and blue carpets became a trend. In the Prince's Chamber, they passed a giant statue of Queen Victoria sat upon her throne and in the House of Lords, another huge golden throne stood for when the sovereign came to pay a visit. Jerome led them down to another huge room, but this room had stone walls, unlike the others which were wood-panelled.

'This is Westminster Hall' Jerome told them 'as you can see it is a lot less fancy than the others and a lot barer. This is one of the oldest parts of the building and is one of the rooms which have survived since the medieval times. This room has been used for lots of different purposes such as grand dinners; coronations and even the trial of guy fawkes. If we enter the gate here and go down these steps we enter St Mary's undercroft' Jerome continued as he led them down into a large underground chapel.

'The chapel was built in twelve ninety-seven by Edward I. St Stephens chapel was used for the royalty to pray in this chapel was for the court and the royal household.' Jack and Alfie stood in awe as they looked up at the impressive ceiling. There were dragons, angels and the heads of man and beasts carved into the wood looking down on them. The floor was marble as were the columns that looked as if they were holding up the ceiling.

'Part of the chapel was once used as a dining room for the speaker of the commons. If you look over here, holes have been bored into the wall for the kitchen chimney. The chapel has also been used as a wine cellar and even was once a stable for Oliver Cromwell's horses. More recently though it has been reinstated as a chapel and is still used today for ceremonies, some of our parliament members have been married here and some have had their children christened here.'

'Really?' Henry asked.

'Yes, Stanley had his son christened here a few years ago' Jerome replied. 'Anyway, I think it's time for a toilet break. Shall we take 10?'

Alfie darted into the end cubicle and carefully took his backpack off and placed it on the floor before unzipping it and gently removing the hand mirror.

'Are you enjoying yourself' he whispered at Meritamen.

'Oh yes' she smiled 'I don't remember most of the rooms as they have changed so much since I was last here. But I remember Elizabeth taking me to a ball that was being held in her honour in Westminster Hall and that room has hardly changed at all' she grinned.

'Where would you like to go next?' Alfie asked.

'I was once placed into storage in the Jewel Tower. It would be interesting to see how that has changed over the years' Meritamen replied.

'Ok, the Jewel Tower it is' Alfie smiled down at her as he placed her back into his backpack.

Jerome greeted them with a grin as they returned from their toilet breaks.

'Right boys, shall we explore the Jewel tour next and then return to your father's office, were I shall order up some lunch for us?' he asked.

'Sounds splendid' Henry laughed as his stomach gave a loud growl.

'Great follow me' Jerome chuckled. He led Alfie, Jack and Henry out of the main building and around the back of the grounds towards the Abbey that stood next door. Alfie suddenly noticed a small iron gate tucked away in the bushes as they turned down a narrow path. Jerome opened the gate and led them through into a large and beautiful garden. There were flowers of every sort and a huge apple tree loomed over them.

'I like to refer to this as the secret garden' Jerome smiled as he leant down and picked up an apple off the ground. 'You need to try these they are delicious' he added before taking a large bite.

'I love apples' beamed Henry as he mimicked his boss and took a large bite out of a glossy red apple he had just picked up off the ground.

'Think I'll pass thanks' mumbled Alfie as he looked on in disgust.

'Same' replied Jack.

'Your loss' Jerome shrugged as he led his tour group through the grounds of the private garden and towards a small stone building that lay on its edge. 'This is the Jewel Tower' he said, gesturing up at the building as they approached. 'Built in thirteen sixty-five, on land that at the time belonged to the nearby Westminster Abbey. It was built to house the King's private collection of treasures. If you look where you are standing you can see the remains of what was once a moat which surrounded the whole building.'

Alfie and Jack looked down at their feet and suddenly realised they were stood in a large dent in the grass.

'The building is three storeys high and was built with ninety-eight boatloads of ragstone that was shipped here from Maidstone. The building in its later life was used as a wardrobe for the kings and queens who resided at Westminster and now it is open to the public for tours. Follow me' said Jerome as he led the boys, threw the door of the Jewel Tower. 'Pretty big wardrobe don't you think?' he giggled before showing them the unrestored fourteenth-century vault which stood inside the building.

'That was a great tour' beamed Jack as they remerged back into the sunny garden.

'Thank you so much Mr Calvin' Alfie added, looking up at the man's smiling face.

'Oh please, call me Jerome. You are both very welcome, although it is I who should be thanking you. I have had a very fun morning and here was me on the tube earlier thinking how dull the day ahead would be.' The four of them laughed at Jerome's comment as they headed back up to the main building.

Once they had all arrived back at Henry's office, Jerome once again picked up the phone that sat upon the desk and called Mary to order some lunch. Before long the office door opened and a man walked in with a silver trolley full of plates of hamburgers, chips, salad and biscuits. The four of them sat in silence as they stuffed their faces.

'Well once again compliments to the chef' beamed Jerome as he wiped his mouth with a napkin.

'Well I am full and happy' smiled Henry 'I really appreciate you taking the morning off to show us around sir' he added.

'Not at all Henry, not at all the pleasure is mine' Jerome replied, shaking his head 'sadly though my fun is over. I must return to my office and suffer the raff of poor Mary after she has had to cancel all my appointments. How that woman puts up with my naughtiness I do not know; she is a god send.' He chuckled before saying his goodbyes and leaving the room.

'Your boss is so cool' Alfie giggled.

'He is a very nice man, isn't he' Henry replied. 'Ok, shall we clear up our lunch and head over to Big Ben before we go home?'

'Yes please' beamed Jack.

****

Alfie, Jack and Henry stood outside a small wooden door with a sign on it which read "clock tower" in golden letters. Henry opened the door and proceeded to read some facts about the tower to the boys off of a leaflet he had picked up from the entrance hall, as they began the mammoth climb up the staircase.

'The tower is two hundred and five feet tall with three hundred and thirty-four steps. It was built in eighteen fifty-nine and in two thousand and twelve, it was renamed Elizabeth tower after our current queen. The bell that chimes at the top of the tower is called the Great Bell but is more fondly referred to as Big Ben.' After one hundred and fourteen steps, the two boys and their father stood gasping for air in a small room.

'This is called the prison room' Henry read aloud once he had caught his breath. 'So-called because in eighteen eighty, an MP was kept here overnight as punishment for his antisocial behaviour.'

'What did he do?' Asked Alfie.

'Well, when an MP gets elected they have to first swear the loyalty to the crown before they can undertake any of their duties.' Henry explained 'Years ago the Bible was used, so you would place your hand on the Bible and swear your loyalty to the king or queen. This MP stated that he was an Atheist and that he didn't want to swear in on the Bible. He was refused any other way and was asked to leave the building. He then became quite unruly and disruptive and so security threw him in here for the night so he could calm down. From that day on this room has been referred to as the prison room.'

'What an idiot' shrugged Jack as they all began to climb back up the steps towards the giant bell at the top.

The view from behind the glass of Big Bens giant face was truly awesome. The two boys and their father stood in silence for a few minutes and looked out as far as the eye could see.

CHAPTER FIFTEEN

'Did you have fun?' Rose asked her two sons as they burst through the front door.

'It was the best mum. The Prime minister showed us around it was so cool' gasped Jack

'And he got us burgers and chips for lunch, so we didn't eat the lunch you made us, sorry' Alfie informed her.

'Never mind seems you had dinner for lunch we can have lunch for dinner' Rose smiled as she took the brown paper bags back off each of them. Alfie and Jack turned and flew up the stairs to their room.

'What are they up to?' Rose asked, turning to her husband.

'I have no clue' Henry shrugged.

Alfie and Jack flopped onto their beds. Alfie carefully removed Meritamen's mirror from inside his battered backpack and placed it down in the middle of him and his brother.

'Oh my dear, dear boys' Meritamen smiled as her face appeared in the glass 'I had such a wonderful day. Thank you.'

'You are very welcome' Jack beamed back at her positively thrilled to have made the Queen so happy.

'Did being there bring back any memories?' Alfie asked.

'Oh yes. Lots of happy memories' Meritamen's eyes glazed over as she allowed her memories to wash over her. After a short pause, she smiled at the boys and asked if they were ready for the next part of her tale, to which they both eagerly agreed.

'Now I left the story with Miss Jacobs and Louisa leaving Edington and returning back to England. After a few very choppy days at sea and a few more days of travel via Horse and Carriage, we finally arrived at Staffordshire house and were relieved to find Harriet waiting for our arrival having received our letter a day earlier. Harriet welcomed Miss Jacobs and Louisa with open arms and her look of relief to finally reunite with me was plain to see. Once her guests were settled, she took me into her chambers and asked me about the sights I had witnessed. I ensured I left nothing out. Harriet was horrified; she had not realised just how bad the situation in America was. Over the next few days Harriet, Miss Jacobs and Louisa worked franticly; they had meetings with parliament members, interviews with local newspapers and wrote letter after letter to the White House. Eventually, a letter came from President Lincoln himself asking Miss Jacobs to return to America and set up residence in Washington where her influence would be much appreciated. A few weeks later, Miss Jacobs and Louisa left England and returned to America and I stayed with Harriet. As the months passed, we kept in touch with Miss Jacobs via letter. She informed us in eighteen sixty-five that slavery had been abolished in all of America's states and a lot of the states had welcomed the news while others fought against it. Miss Jacobs continued to work hard to rehabilitate former slaves and to help keep people safe against the rebels. Then one day in the March of eighteen ninety-seven, we received a letter from Louisa to inform us that Harriet Jacobs had died on the seventh day of that month. Louisa then took over her mother's work and continued to support those whom needed her help.'

'What an amazing women' Alfie gasped in awe.

'She really was, and she taught me so much.'

'So, what did you do next?' asked Jack.

'Well, I had stayed with Harriet and she had her hands full with looking after the queen. Whilst I had been in America Prince Albert had died and the queen had gone into deep mourning. Her depression had consumed her and she had grown rather fat and lazy. Harriet was the only person who the queen seemed to listen to and so she was summoned by the queen's house staff whenever Victoria was acting difficult, which seemed to be more often than not. Harriet threw herself into caring for her dear friend, but one night in October eighteen sixty-eight she fell asleep in her home, Stafford house and never woke. Victoria was beside herself yet again. I stayed with the queen for a while after Harriet's passing, but not even I could pull Victoria out of her slump and soon her depression spread to me. I had seen so many terrible things and lost so many wonderful people and before I knew it, I was back in the darkness of my mirror hiding from the outside world. I couldn't even tell you how I ended up in possession of Mrs Gordon, or how many years had passed; if any. But I remember a feeling as if I was awaking from a deep sleep; I could hear muffled voices around me and the darkness began to get lighter. The first thing I remember is looking around the part of the room that I could see and wondering where on earth am I. The room was spacious and light and a beautiful, elegant lady with flaming red hair swept across the room in a flowing gown. That was my first glimpse of Lucy. I ventured out of the darkness more often after that and would watch this intriguing woman while taking care not to show myself. I soon discovered that Lucy was a fashion artist and a good one at that. She was one of the first global fashion brands with shop's in, London, New York, Paris and Chicago and a string of famous clients including actresses, dancers and royalty. I would often listen in on her conversations and I have to say I was sceptical of her plans to start up the very first catwalk show but as history would go on to prove it was a splendid idea. Lucy was the wife of a rich Scottish landowner and sportsman named Cosmo Duff Gordon. He was a very handsome man with a fabulous moustache that I am sure took him hours each morning to wax into its perfect state. I watched Lucy work hard daily designing and then producing beautiful lingerie and gowns and training her models.

She really was a fantastic businesswoman and had been working hard on her spring collection, which she was making arrangements to take to her shop in New York. One morning in April of Nineteen twelve we travelled via a new invention; a car, to Southampton. I had been carefully placed into Lucy's handbag for although I had not revealed myself to her, she knew I was of great value and so always kept me close at hand; I was her most prized possession. I will never forget the first time the Titanic came into my view. Lucy had taken me out of her bag only for a second to check her lipstick was not smudged and my eyes were stuck on the massive ship that towered behind her. I had never seen anything like it before, and I gathered by the number of reporters and spectators who were crowded around that I wasn't the only one. So this is the unsinkable titanic, I heard Lucy state to her husband as we stepped on board. Our first-class cabin was utterly stunning. Much different to the previous ships I had travelled on with Miss Jacobs. Our cabin was very large and one could be fooled to think they were stood in a drawing-room of a country estate. The walls of the cabin appeared to be wood with gold gilding, large couches were positioned around beautifully crafted fireplaces; there were electric heaters in the lounge area and beautiful pink curtains over the windows. The bedroom was separate from the lounge and held a large four-poster bed. Each first-class suite had a telephone and a bell so guests could summon their personal steward. Some first-class suites even had their own promenade, although ours did not. The first three nights we were on board were pleasant. Lucy and Cosmo mingled with other wealthy and influential first-class passengers. We attended fine dining events and church masses, strolled around the ship's huge deck, and dined with the captain. We met many colourful characters, my favourite being Molly Brown. Molly was an American woman whose husband had struck gold in Colorado. As she was referred to as new money, some of the other first-class passengers looked down their nose at her, but I found her quite charming. It was our fourth night at sea when disaster struck. Lucy and Cosmo had not long got into bed when the ship suddenly gave a large shudder and a loud rumble followed. Lucy jumped out of bed in a panic and Cosmo followed they put on their dressing gowns and peered out of the cabin door and into the corridor to discover they were not the only people to have heard the noise. After a few minutes, the staff appeared calmly and began to hand out lifejackets while reassuring us that all was well, but that we should make our way up to the deck. Lucy began to panic, and Cosmo tried his best to reassure her. I remember Lucy walking out onto the deck and the sound of violins hitting us and Cosmo saying look Lucy if there really was something to worry about, I am sure the band would not be playing.

A rather official steward shouted for the women and children to get into lifeboats. Cosmo ushered Lucy over to a hectic queue that was forming on the far end of the ship. This was when I knew that something serious was going on. Why do we need to get into lifeboats if everything is fine? Lucy became rather frantic in fact, everyone became very frantic. The ship's deck was full of terrified people pushing past each other, shouting for their loved ones, children crying. It was horrible; Lucy was so scared she was violently shaking with fear. I peered threw my glass and saw an elderly woman refusing to get onto a lifeboat, her frantic husband begging her to go and she refused to leave his side. Women everywhere sobbing and kissing farewell to their husbands who were ensuring them they would get the next boat, children screaming as they were ripped from their fathers and lowered into the little wooden lifeboats with their mothers. I overheard a steward asking why the lifeboats were not filled, only to be told that staff were worried they would sink if loaded to the max and the steward responded with, well there isn't enough of them anyway. Lucy heard this too and her panic began to rise she and Cosmo ran to the other end of the deck which was a little less crowded, we passed the ships banned as we ran who were still playing their violins, trying desperately to soothe the panicked passengers with music. We arrived at the lifeboat as it was being filled with passengers Lucy turned to Cosmo with tears running down her cheeks and wrapped her arms around him, refusing to leave him. A steward inside the boat informed them that he was about to lower the craft and they best jump in quick if they wanted to live. Lucy grabbed Cosmos hand and they both entered the boat. Before long we had hit the icy water and began to row away, even though our boat which could fit forty people in only had twelve.

Being out in the middle of the Atlantic in the dead of night is the airiest place I have ever been, the air was that cold Lucy exhaled what looked like a large amount of smoke with every breath. It was deadly silent, nobody spoke, faintly in the distance, the screams could be heard from the doomed ship we had just escaped. And then to our absolute horror we watched as the back of the ship rose into the air, the whole ship looked as if it was almost diagonal and then it split, it split right in half and slowly began to submerge into the sea. We could see people jumping into the ocean and franticly trying to swim away before the force of the ship dragged them too, to their watery graves. We need to go back I cried, we need to save them, but my voice was ignored. Everybody on our lifeboat turned their faces and continued to row into the night. I sunk back into the darkness off my mirror, refusing to witness anymore.'

'That is awful' gasped Alfie 'why didn't they go back to help?'

'Well would you? I am not for one moment suggesting that they did the right thing, for what it is worth I think they should have gone back, but that is easy for me to say. I have been around for hundreds of years; I have lived an exceptional life and if I had sank that day, then I would have laid at the bottom of the ocean for years maybe forever, but I would not have died. You see all those poor souls freezing to death in the ocean; there was hundred of them, thousands even. What do you think they would have done if a small, little boat had sailed over to them? Chances are they would have swarmed it. The people in the lifeboats were terrified and a lot of them received backlash for not going back to help, but are they guilty? After all, all they did was survive. I don't think anyone could argue that they would not have done the same, how could one possibly know how they would act in that situation if one had not been there.'

'Yeah I suppose your right' Alfie agreed.

'As I previously stated, I recoiled back into the confines of my mirror and refused to witness any more of what was happening around me. Therefore, I could not tell you what unfolded on that lifeboat, all I remember is peering out of my glass a few days, maybe weeks later and I was inside an apartment in New York city. Lucy was pacing up and down and having a heated argument with Cosmo about an upcoming court case they were facing. I soon discovered that the court hearing was regarding a conversation that was supposed to have happened on lifeboat one. On that boat was Lucy, Cosmo, Franks (Lucy's maid) and crew members from the ship. Apparently one of the crew members made a comment about how his livelihood was on the ship and he was in despair of having lost everything, Cosmo apparently gave each of the crew members Five pounds. Once they had safely arrived in New York the story was changed, and it was implied that Cosmo had paid each of the Crew members five pounds to not return to the sinking ship to save the doomed passengers. I could not tell you which of these stories are true, but I can tell you that the court found them not guilty of the latter. However, the scandal haunted them for the rest of their lives.

Cosmo and Lucy grew apart after the scandal, Cosmo retreated from society and spent most of his remaining time in his estate in Aberdeen. Lucy, however, refused to let anything get in her way and so she pushed forward with her dressmaking career. Before long she was dressing the stars of Hollywood and the courtesans of Paris. But soon Lucy changed, she became completely self-obsessed, if she was in an elevator nobody else was allowed in with her, her staff would have to tip-toe around the office as not to distract 'the genius' as she worked. She sacked her closest business partner and friend Edward Molyneux as he urged her to change her fashion with the times, and soon her business crumbled. Her fashion became outdated and Lucy found herself bankrupt. I was sold to an antique store in New York to pay for her travel back to London, so she could spend her final years with her daughter Esme.'

'I don't know how I feel about this woman; I don't know if I like her or not' said Jack.

'Well I don't blame you' Meritamen laughed. 'But you can not deny she was an amazing woman. She came from nothing and worked hard to achieve what she did, but sadly fame and power consumed her and was ultimately her downfall.'

'So, what happened to you after that?' Alfie asked.

'Well, I stayed in the antique shop for a few years until one day a lovely young woman came in and took a fancy to my mirror. She purchased me and that is where my story continues.'

'Boys, its time for tea' Rose called up the stairs.

'Sorry Meritamen we have to go now. Can you tell us the rest later?' Asked Jack.

'Of course, dear' Smiled the Queen as the two boys placed her back inside the drawer and left the room.

CHAPTER SIXTEEN

The boys were greeted by their mother at the bottom of the stairs.

'Picnic in the garden for tea tonight boys' she smiled before leading her two sons out into the back garden where their father sat waiting on a large blue, checked picnic rug. A tasty feast lay over the rug which included the boy's uneaten lunch from earlier that day. They sat down and dug in.

'How is the job search going darling?' Henry asked Rose through a mouthful of Tuna sandwich.

'Actually, it's going great' Rose grinned. 'I have a second job interview in the Victoria and Albert museum tomorrow afternoon. I received the call this morning; they seem rather keen.'

'That's fantastic mum' beamed Alfie. 'What does the job entail?'

'Well I don't want to get too excited as it is early days but, it is sort of my dream job' his mother giggled. 'That's all I am saying for now. I really don't want to get my hopes up.'

'I have every confidence in you dear' Henry smiled as he leaned over and gave his wife a reassuring hug.

The family continued to chat away about the boy's upcoming visit to their new school and days out the family had planned. After finishing their picnic, the family enjoyed a football game in the garden before Rose sent the boys upstairs to get baths.

Alfie and Jack soon found themselves back in their beds, ready to hear the next part of Meritamens tale.

'I was purchased in an antique store in New York, by a lovely young woman named Helen Fairchild' Meritamen continued. 'Helen had come from Pennsylvania, where she lived and worked on her family farm with her parents and six siblings. She had trained as a nurse and one month after America declared that they were to join the fight in Europe, also known as world war one, she had volunteered to go overseas to be a nurse on the front line. Her first port of call was to travel from New York to Liverpool, England. It was on the ship to Liverpool that I chose to reveal myself to Helen as I had taken a liking to this young lady almost instantly. She was of a strong character and did not show any sign of fear when my face first appeared into the glass. I introduced myself and briefly told my story to which she replied with hers. Helen informed me that the year was nineteen seventeen and that we should arrive in Liverpool on the twenty-sixth of May. After a few days at sea, we arrived in Liverpool on the date expected. Liverpool was a very busy city with a large dock that traded goods all over the world. The city was mostly comprised of areas of slums, although there were areas of great wealth due to the number of business tycoons making this city their homes to take advantage of the trading docks.

Helen checked into a truly stunning hotel right in the heart of the city called the Adelphi hotel, but our stay was short as our true destination was the Countries capital. And so, after a day of rest we departed from Liverpool and made our way to London.

We arrived at the Waldorf Hotel in London on the second of June. Helen spent a lot of her free time writing letters to her parents and siblings back home. She did not take me outside often but would always take me out of her bag the second she arrived back to her room, to tell me of all that had happened that day. I was grateful for the company after spending so many years alone.

By the end of June, we had arrived in France and Helen was sent to the Pennsylvania base hospital number ten at Le Treport. She soon volunteered to spend what she thought was a few days on the front line in Flanders. She did not take much of her belongings with her due to her belief that she would be returning soon, but she would not part with me and so I was placed in her bag along with two of her uniforms. We arrived at the tent that would be our home for the next many days. Helen carefully placed me and the rest of her belongings under her camp bed and headed straight out to get to work. She was a determined young woman with a very big heart. She never once complained that it constantly rained every day, or that she had to wade through mud everywhere she went. She told me once that the operating tent on the front line was ankle-deep in mud and she felt sorry for the doctors who had to stand in it all day. The hospital base that Helen worked at had sixty-four American nurses to around two thousand soldiers. One day after some particularly heavy bombing, six hundred soldiers were brought to be treated in less than forty-eight hours, and this continued for some days. Helen was exhausted and what was originally supposed to be a few days soon turned into a few months, the demand for nurses on the front line was so desperate and overwhelming that Helen could not leave. The front line was a very dangerous place to be and we were often exposed to heavy shelling and attacks of mustard gas. One evening around Christmas Helen returned to her tent and informed me how she had been treating a soldier when mustard gas was dropped on her tent, in her panic and concern for the soldier's safety she had given him her gas mask. Soon Helen became seriously ill, what had started out as tonsillitis had developed into crippling abdominal pain and vomiting. Helen was sent for an x-ray which showed a large ulcer in her stomach. It was decided that Helen should be operated on immediately. The operation at first appeared to be a success, but a couple of days later, Helen fell into a coma and sadly died. It is believed the mustard gas had either caused the ulcer or made it considerably worse and that unknown complications from the operation had eventually been her ending. She was buried with full military honours in a cemetery in Le Treport.'

'She was a true veteran, wasn't she' sighed Alfie. 'What an amazing woman.'

'She really was' smiled Meritamen. 'I was found among her items by a fellow nurse who had planned on returning me via airmail to Helen's family, but I was lost among the thousands of parcels in the mailroom and soon found myself in a post office in Germany.

Know it is time for you two to get some sleep. I will continue my story tomorrow.' Smiled the Queen lovingly at the two young boys as they struggled to keep their eyes open. Alfie lazily nodded in response and placed the mirror back into the bedside draw before collapsing onto his pillow and falling into a deep sleep along with his brother.

CHAPTER SEVENTEEN

The next morning Alfie and Jack woke to the smell of maple syrup floating up the staircase and to their noses. Groggily they made their way down the stairs and into the kitchen to be greeted by their mother and father and a large plate of pancakes.

'How did you sleep guys?' Rose asked as she leaned over and gave them each a morning kiss on the top of their heads.

'Great' grinned Jack. 'What time is your interview mum?'

'It's at five; your father is going to leave work early and come home, so you're not alone.'

'Actually' Grinned Henry 'I am not going to work today. I have taken the day off so you can get all your interview prep done. I am going to take these two little terrors out, so they aren't getting in your way.'

'We never get in the way' protested Alfie in a mocking tone.

'Thank you so much' beamed Rose. 'I knew there was a reason I married you' she giggled.

'So, what's the plan dad?' Asked Jack excitedly.

'I was thinking the Tower of London?' Henry asked, knowing full well what the answer would be. Alfie and Jack jumped from their chairs and ran around the kitchen excitedly.

'I think that's a yes' laughed their mother.

After filling their stomachs with pancakes and maple syrup, the two brothers quickly washed, dressed and stood impatiently waiting at the front door for their father.

'Good luck today sweetie' Henry whispered to Rose as he pulled her in towards him for a tight hug. 'You will be fine, and I will be back before you leave to reassure you some more' he smiled. 'Right you two I take it you're ready to go' he said, turning to his two sons.

'We sure are' beamed Alfie excitedly.

Alfie, Jack and their father headed out of the house and jumped into Henrys Jeep. After what felt like forever driving through the busy morning traffic, they arrived at the car park for the Tower of London. They paid for their tickets and booked on for a tour with a tour guide called Ariel. Ariel was a middle, aged man who had clearly dedicated his life to London history; the family were really impressed with the tour. After an hour, Ariel told them to take a quick break to get a snack, which the family welcomed.

'What do you think guys?' Henry asked.

'It's amazing. I can not believe this place has been used for so many different things, a zoo, a prison, a home. The history here is fantastic' beamed Alfie.

'Ariel is so clever' gasped Jack. 'I think he probably knows everything about everything.'

'I am sure he does' Henry giggled.

After their break, Ariel returned and took the family over to the jewel tower so they could see the crown jewels. Alfie and Jack were very excited, although a little scared at the high level of security that surrounded the Queen's jewels.

'Shall we get some ice-cream from the café before we head home then?' Asked Henry once the tour was over.

'Yes please, and thanks for a great day dad' Alfie replied.
******

Henry and his sons returned home with the remains of their chocolate ice-creams around their mouths.

'Fun day?' Rose laughed as she licked her thumb and attempted to wipe away the stains from around Jack's lips as he protested and grunted.

'Get off me mum! Urgh that's gross'

'It was amazing mum. How did your interview prep go? Are you feeling confident?' Alfie asked.

'Yes, I think I am going to be ok' she smiled. She looked down at her watch before informing them all that she had to leave. She quickly kissing each of their cheeks, grabbing her briefcase and raced out the door.

'Looks like pizza for tea' Henry replied as he made his way into the kitchen and began rooting around in the drawers for a takeaway pamphlet.

'Ok dad. Can you call us when it's here? We are just going to have a chill in our room' Alfie called as he made his way up the staircase.

'Yeah, it's been a busy day' added Jack as he followed his brother towards the bedroom they shared. Henry mumbled some sort of agreeable reply, as he continued rooting.

'Meritamen?' Alfie whispered as he carefully took the mirror from out of its hiding place.

'Hello' the Queen replied with a smile as her face appeared into the glass. 'How was your day?'

'Really good. We went to the Tower of London with dad. Mum has gone for a job interview in the Victoria and Albert museum and she needed some quiet time, so dad took us out.'

'That sounds fantastic. Did you enjoy yourselves?' Meritamen replied.

'Yes, it was great' said Alfie.

'Would you like to hear the rest of my story now?'

'Oh yes please' The boys replied as they got comfortable on Jacks bed.

'Where was I up to? Oh yes, I remember. I had gotten lost in the post I found myself in a German post office in what would be the equivalent of a lost and found bin. A young man working in the post office happened to come across me one day and placed me into his satchel. Once he had finished his shift, he hopped onto a pedal bike and road to a house in Forchtenberg. Once he arrived at his destination, he parked his bike against a nearby railing and knocked on the door of a townhouse. A kind-looking man with a funny moustache answered the door and beamed at the young man before welcoming him into his home. A baby girl lay in a Moses basket in the corner of the living room that the young postal worker had just been guided into. The young man smiled down at the new-born and shook the older man's hand to congratulate him. He then reached into his satchel and carefully taking out the mirror he placed it into the bottom of the baby's basket.

I soon discovered the child was called Sophie Scholl; she was a German girl; her father was a politician. They were a nice family and were very close. Sophies older brother Hans was very protective of his younger sister and the two grew to be very close. I was Sophie's favourite plaything, although I did not appreciate her using me as a teething ring, I was still very fond of her. Sophie would scream her cot down if I was removed from it and so her parents would leave my mirror at the bottom of her cot most nights. If the child woke, I would appear in my mirror and sing the songs of the goddess Hathor to her to help her drift back off to sleep. As Sophie grew older, I became her secret fairy godmother, only Hans knew of my identity and I would often keep the two of them up late telling my stories.

In nineteen thirty-three a man named Adolf Hitler became chancellor of Germany with his Nazi party (a year later in nineteen thirty-four his title changed to Fuhrer). He ordered that all children must attend a sort of special school. The girl's wing of the Hitler youth was called Bund Deutscher madel which translates into the league of German girls. Sophie was twelve when she joined. I was concerned about some of the things she would come home and tell me, it was clear she was being filled with propaganda and her father realised this too. He and his political party became Anti-Nazi politicians. I tried my best to keep Sophie grounded and not allow herself to become brainwashed. Then one evening in nineteen thirty-seven Hans and his friends were out at a German youth movement group that they were members of. The German youth movement was sort of like your version of scouts, but the Nazi party had made such groups illegal. Hans and his friends were arrested, and Sophie was beside herself. This enforced Sophies already sceptical doubts of the propaganda she was being fed. A couple of nights later, Sophie came to me and said she had heard about a Roman Catholic bishop who was holding an anti-Nazi sermon and she wanted us to go. She placed me in her satchel, and we headed off. The sermon was powerful, and the priest preached 'the theology of the conscience' which struck a chord with Sophie and her uneasy feeling towards Hitler and his regime grew stronger inside of her.

In nineteen forty-seven Sophie enrolled in the University of Munich to study Biology and Philosophy. Her brother Hans already attended the university and so Sophie would spend her free time with him and his friends. The group had strong political views and an even stronger dislike towards Hitler and the Nazi regime they often talked about doing something, but they weren't sure what. What followed can only be described as a domino effect, Sophie and Hans received a call from their frantic mother who informed them that their father had been imprisoned by the Gestapo (Nazi police) because he had been overheard calling Hitler 'the scrounge of humanity'. Soon after that, their friend Fritz Hartnager returned from his compulsory trip to the eastern front where he had been forced to work and told them of the horrors he had seen. He informed us that there were mass killings of Jews in work camps and that they were being forced to live in ghettos, where the living conditions were so poor many were dying. Fritz told us that in one ghetto he had come across, the price of one loaf of bread was three hundred marks, which was then the equivalent of eighty American dollars. He also told us how he had witnessed with his own eyes soviet prisoners of war being shot in mass graves. We felt sick and my mind slipped back to my time spent in Edington. How can humans be so evil towards each other? I urged Sophie and Hans to do something, but to be honest, they did not need much urging. They were infuriated and disgusted. They believed that if more people knew the truth of what was really happening, then the country would rally together and put a stop to it. They decided to form a group with other like-minded young people, and they named this group 'The White Rose'. They made pamphlets denouncing the Nazis and urging Germany's people to fight against and resist the regime. Sophie purchased an illegal typewriter and typed their arguments urging others to join them and find ways to resist Hitler and his party.

One afternoon while scattering their sixth pamphlet around Munich's university with her brother, they were spotted by the janitor who informed the Gestapo. Sophie and Hans were arrested, Sophie at first denied everything until her brother pleaded guilty and then to ensure he did not receive all the punishment alone, Sophie also confessed. They took full responsibility to ensure nobody else from the white rose were discovered.

Sophie and Hans were imprisoned ready to await trial. I was confiscated along with Sophie's satchel by a Gestapo member, who instantly realised my value and sold me later that day to an antique store for one hundred marks. I did not discover Sophie's fate until many years later when the war was over, and Hitler was overthrown. Annie was holidaying in Germany and happened to come across the antique store, which still stood untouched and owned by the same family. When I showed myself to Annie and told her my story, she made it her mission to discover Sophie's fate and that she did. Annie discovered that Sophie attended her trial on February twenty-second nineteen forty-three. She was found guilty and was executed by means of beheading with a guillotine that same afternoon at five o'clock. It is widely reported that Sophie showed great courage as she made her final walk down to her execution and her final words were recorded by the prison staff. "How can we expect righteousness to prevail when there is hardly anyone willing to give himself up individually to a righteous cause? Such a fine, sunny day and I have to go, but what does my death matter, if through us, thousands of people are awakened and stirred to action?"

After Sophie and Hans death, a copy of the sixth pamphlet was smuggled out of Germany and given to the allies. The pamphlet was renamed "The manifesto of the students on Munich" and the allies printed millions of copies which they used to try and recruit German people to fight against Hitler. And so, I take comfort from knowing that Sophie and Hans did not die in vain.

I have already explained how Annie came across me. She then brought me back to England to this house, and I stayed here with her and her family. As Annie got older, her mind became confused and her memories began to fade and it was around that time that I found myself inside that dreaded old trunk until you found me. So that children brings us full circle.' Smiled Meritamen.

'That was the best story ever!!' Exclaimed Jack.

'We really appreciate you telling us' smiled Alfie. 'Sophie was an amazing woman wasn't she' he added in awe.

'She certainly was. In fact, she is probably my favourite owner' Meritamen replied with a sad look in her eyes.

Suddenly the children could hear noises from downstairs that informed them that their mother had returned.

'Our mum is home and she's had a really important afternoon, so we are going to see how she got on' explained Alfie.

'We will be back in a second' added Jack as they ran out of the door. Downstairs mum and the pizza had arrived at the same time and the family headed into the kitchen.

'How did your interview go mum?' asked Alfie.

'I got the job' beamed Rose. 'I mean it's a little scary, they want me to teach classes on the history of the English monarchy. It's going to mean doing a lot of research, I mean I know a lot already but teaching high school lessons and teaching one pacific topic to adults is a completely different ball game.'

'You will do fine' Henry beamed. 'I am so proud of you.'

Alfie and Jack glanced at each other as if they had both had an idea at the same time. Jack gave his brother a little nod and Alfie excused himself from the table and darted up the stairs to his room.

'Well mum, Alfie and I have something that could help you with that, but you have to promise not to scream'. Rose turned to her son with a look of confusion etched across her face. Within seconds Alfie had returned and now he and Jack stood in front of their parents looking a mixture of excited and terrified.

'What is going on?' Henry asked his sons.

'It is best if we show you rather than try and explain' Alfie replied as he held up a beautiful, expensive-looking hand mirror.

'Good evening Mr and Mrs Ashton, I am Queen Meritamen of Egypt'

Rose and Henry's jaws dropped open as they stared at the face in the mirror.

Printed in Great Britain
by Amazon

57913845R00078